THOSE TWO OLD CAMPING BROADS ARE AT IT AGAIN

Karen J. Bates

Ordering Information:

For orders and inquiries, please contact:
1-888-375-9818
www.toplinkpublishing.com
bookorder@toplinkpublishing.com

Printed in the United States of America

Prologue

This novel is a sequel to "Camping Experiences of Two Old Broads."

There were two friends who tent camped together for many years. As they grew older they found that tent camping was a chore so decided to purchase a fifth wheel recreational vehicle together. Marie had retired as a social worker and Jane's career was in commercial property management. When Jane retired, they decided to travel across the country and managed to get into some precarious situations along the way. However, many wonderful things also happened and one was that they met their sweethearts. Marie married Vince Lechendyke and moved out to his ranch in Albuquerque, New Mexico. Jane decided she just wasn't ready to take that big step yet. She has finally changed her mind and she proposes to Nick but a catastrophe happens. Now the story continues.

Chapter One

I t was a nice warm evening and Jane was enjoying her backyard deck. It was a two-tiered redwood with beautiful accent lighting and decorative brick walls. The contractors had recently finished building a wood-burning fireplace with gas grill in one corner and a canvas awning by the entrance to the living room.

She was relaxing on the chaise lounge and listening to the rain hitting overhead. It reminded her of her tent camping days with Marie. They would invariably be camping when it rained but was always nice to hear raindrops on the roof of the tent. When they moved on to traveling in their recreational vehicle, they missed hearing those raindrops.

Since Marie had moved to New Mexico, Jane was lost without their traveling. With her A-type personality, she always needed to be busy. Retirement was pretty boring and she pondered what to do with her time.

She decided to go to the country club and see if she could find a tennis player. As she pulled into the parking lot, she saw one of the partners of the former company where she had worked many years.

Jane walked up to him and said, "So good to see you, Fred."

"So, Jane, how long have you been back in town? Are you getting tired of that camping routine?"

"When I started this journey, I had no idea how long I would last before getting bored. You know me and my challenges. Once I conquer them, I find another one; but this camping thing has been a blast. It's so much fun seeing our beautiful country. Marie and I would plan our routes and then see how accurate we would be at figuring mileage, tours, timetable, and such. It was very challenging, but I never got bored. Imagine that! The problem is that Marie got married and moved to New Mexico. It's no longer fun pulling that huge rig by myself. Marie says we will still do some traveling, but nothing like we've been doing these past four years."

Fred said, "I've been thinking of calling you as I've been contemplating a new venture and thought you would be just the right person to get it going. In fact, it's the type of operation that you could even do while on the road."

"Timing is everything, Fred, because I was going to call you and see if you could use a good consultant. Let's go into the club and discuss it further."

"I would love to do that, Jane, but I'm meeting my tennis partner in about ten minutes. How about meeting me in my office tomorrow at 10:00AM. I'll have the other partners there also. They'll be glad to see you again."

"That sounds like a plan, Fred. Have a great tennis match."

She managed to find a tennis partner who had been on one of her leagues and they had fun playing a few sets. Afterward, she showered in the locker room, dressed, and made her way out to the parking lot. The rain had stopped and gave a nice fresh smell in the air.

As Jane was driving home, she thought of how blessed she was to have had a wonderful career and great people to work with. She was intrigued with Fred's idea and wondered just what type of venture it was.

As she drove into her driveway, her cell phone rang. It was Marie calling. She said, "Vince is going on a business trip for a few weeks and I thought it would be fun for us to go on one of our travels."

"Wow, Marie. I was ready to call you and see how you were doing. I really miss our travels. However, there is a teeny problem. I was at the country club this evening and ran into one of the partners at the company where I worked. He said it was great to see me again and wondered if I would be interested in working on a venture that the partners have devised. I'm meeting all of them tomorrow to see what's involved. Fred did say that I could even do the work while traveling. You know that I can't just sit around the house and do nothing and this sounds like a wonderful opportunity."

"I'm so happy for you, Jane; but do you really think that you can perform effectively in a full-time job and travel too?"

"I don't envision it being a full-time job, but I'll get clarification when I meet with the partners."

"Let's get back to Vince's business trip. He said that he could drop me off in Cleveland next Monday. I would like to visit with my sister for a few days. I was thinking we could take off on our next journey by the end of next week. Would that be too soon?"

"I'll know better after tomorrow's meeting. We can at least plan where we would like to go. Do you have any ideas?"

Marie said, "We haven't hit the western states. Vince said his trip will probably be about two-three weeks. How about ending at my home in New Mexico. The only problem with that idea is getting you back to Ohio. I guess you could either drive the rig back by yourself or fly home from Albuquerque. I'm sure Vince would have a place to store the rig around this large mountain range of ours."

"How about you two flying here Saturday or Sunday in Vince's jet? We could finalize the details, you can visit your sister, and we could even have an afternoon barbeque with Nick. It would be like old times with the four of us. Vince then could leave next Monday from here on his business trip."

"That sounds like a plan, Jane. I love my husband so much, but this homebody lifestyle is getting pretty boring. I really miss you and our travels. Let me talk to Vince and see if he has any problem with our strategy. By the way, I haven't heard you mention Nick whenever we've talked recently. Are you two back together again?"

Jane pretended there was someone at the front door. "I have to answer the door, Marie. I'll talk to you later. Goodbye."

Marie went into the study and asked Vince, "Have you talked to Nick recently?"

"No, I haven't. I've been meaning to call, but you know how that goes. Why do you ask?"

"I was just talking to Marie about planning an RV trip while you're gone. She mentioned that it would be fun to have a barbeque with the four of us at her house. When I asked if they were together again, she pulled her old trick of someone being at the door and hung up."

"Those two have enough trouble keeping their relationship stable. Let's not meddle in their affairs."

"I don't plan on it. I was just asking if you had heard from Nick. So, is it okay if we fly in your jet to Ohio or were you planning on going commercial jet?"

"I plan on going commercial, but we can take my plane to Cleveland and I can go commercial jet from there."

"That sounds like a lot of trouble, honey. Do you really want to bother?"

"No trouble at all. It's getting late. Let's go to bed."

Chapter Two

The next morning, Jane met with the partners of her former workplace. They presented their ideas to her. Once they finished with the presentation, Jane said, "While it sounds very intriguing, I think I'll pass on the offer. With my working style, I'm afraid that I would be too involved with the project and not have time to enjoy the sites while traveling. I should be back home by mid August. If you're still interested in pursuing this endeavor at that time, please don't hesitate to contact me—that is, if you haven't found someone else by then."

As she was leaving, they thanked her for considering the offer and appreciated her candor, then wished her a safe journey.

That afternoon Jane worked on the itinerary with Illinois being the first stop. Both Jane and Marie had toured many areas of the Midwestern states over the years, so she didn't schedule many activities until they would reach Wyoming. From there, they would go down to Colorado. Jane wanted to spend some time near Denver as she had many friends that she hadn't seen in years. You see, Jane had lived in Colorado for six years and always dreamed of returning one day.

If they had time, they would venture into Utah before heading back to Marie's home in Albuquerque, New Mexico.

The itinerary was scheduled to hook up at a campground every Monday and leave the following Thursday unless they wanted to see more of that particular area. In the event that they didn't like an area, they would just pick up and leave. Ahhh, the joys of RV living.

Once Jane had finished, she called Marie that evening. "I worked all afternoon on our itinerary. With only two months and all of the exciting things that we could see, I'm afraid it's a little aggressive but take a look at it. I just emailed it to you and will look forward to your comments and ideas."

"You always do such a good job of mapping out our trips. They usually are just the right miles for traveling in a day plus the tours are interesting and many times educational. I'm sure it's fine, but I'll look at it just the same. With your new assignment, when do you have us starting this next journey of ours?"

"Actually, I decided against doing the assignment as I'm afraid that I'd get too involved in it and not enjoy our travels."

"I'm glad to hear that as I wondered the same thing. I know your style. You'd dive right in and we'd probably hardly ever tour anything. I'd be reading lots of books and I can do that at home. Thank you, Jane."

"You're welcome. When is Vince leaving on his business trip? Those things will set the stage for when we can get started; but I was thinking of leaving next Thursday."

"He has to be in New York City next Monday. I'll have him land the plane in Cleveland this Saturday. If you still want to have the barbeque, would Sunday afternoon work? If you don't mind, Vince and I would stay at your place Saturday and Sunday. Monday he would take me to my sister's apartment."

"Of course, you two can stay here at my place. How is Hilda doing?"

Marie responded, "She seems to be fine, but I'm sure she has some issues, especially with her Arthritis. Her hands just don't seem to want to work. She can't drive anymore so she has to depend on others and she isn't one to ask for help. The stroke that she had months ago also set her back but fortunately most of her mobility and speech have returned to normal. I feel like I deserted her with me being so far away."

"Hilda would be upset if she heard this conversation, Marie. I talked to her the other day and she is so happy that you found someone to spend the rest of your life with. She is so proud of you. Please don't feel guilty. She has friends to help her and I'm just a phone call away."

"Thank you, Jane, for watching over Hilda for me."

"No thanks are needed. She is a great friend and I enjoy spending time with her. I had better get busy, Marie. I'll talk to you later. Have a fabulous evening and tell Vince I said hello."

"I'll be glad to do that but want to ask how Nick is doing."

"I have to answer the door. I'll tell you later. Goodbye." She then disconnected the cell phone.

Marie thought, *that's the second time she pulled that trick on me.* She wondered if something happened to the relationship with Nick. That sound in Jane's voice was not good so Marie called him.

Marie dialed Nick's cell phone and he answered.

"Marie, it's so good to hear from you. How are the newlyweds doing?"

"We're great and truly lovebirds, Nick, but I'm calling about Jane. I just finished talking to her and when I asked how you were doing, she cut me off and said someone was at the door. She always uses that excuse when she wants to end a conversation on the telephone. In fact, she did it twice in the last two days."

"Well, Marie, she's back to her old, 'I don't want commitment,' style. I am beside myself as I am so much in love with her and have a hard time always leaving her. I'm so frustrated and don't know what to do. I've tried ending our relationship but then I'm more miserable than when we are together. Do you have any suggestions?"

"As a matter of fact, I do. She and I are planning another trip; and leaving next week for a two-month tour of the western states. Let me work on her for you. I can't promise anything. Just let me say this. She is so much in love with you and knows that she will be losing you if she doesn't get her act together."

"Thank you, Marie. On another note, how is that old man of yours doing these days?"

"That's why Jane and I are going on another adventure. He has a business trip starting next Monday and will be gone for a few weeks. I sure have missed our trips and can't wait to get back on the road again. Every time I say that, I think of how we always played that song whenever we started a trip. It was a tradition.

Memories are so wonderful, especially as we get older and not able to do the things we used to do. This body of mine looks and feels like it's 80 years old but my mind tries to tell me that I'm 20. Funny how that works. I guess I should be fortunate that I'm able to do the things I do in my golden years."

"I'm, sure Vince would say that your body is fine, Marie. Please give him my best; and I'll look forward to hearing of your success with my sweetheart. Please take care of yourself."

"You do also, Nick. Goodbye."

Chapter Three

Marie studied the itinerary that Jane had mapped out. She knew Jane used a national camping directory as it gave a volume of information. It would show the entertainment and tours in the area, the amenities of a particular campground, cost, site location, size, etc. Seeing the plans for Wyoming, Colorado, and Utah was really getting Marie excited as she had never been to any of those states.

She called Jane and said, "This looks pretty good Jane. While it may be a little aggressive, we usually accomplished most of the things you had planned. Let's give it a go and see what happens."

"I agree that it's aggressive. I always want to see everything that's in the area, but invariably we have to cut something out or we don't make our timeline. When you arrive Saturday, we can dissect it in more detail. Do you need me to get you and Vince at the airport?"

"That won't be necessary. Vince will be renting a car so we won't be bugging you for wheels all the time."

"Since I'm retired, I don't go out a lot, so my car is available whenever you need it."

"Thank you. You're so sweet, but Vince wants his own wheels. I guess it's a guy thing."

"Okay. Right now, the plan is have you two arrive Saturday afternoon and spend that evening and Sunday night here. Then Vince can take you to your sister's on Monday. I'll plan the barbeque for Sunday afternoon. I need to call Nick. He's been stand offish lately and I don't know what's bugging him."

"Did you ever think that it was you, Jane?"

"Are you lecturing me again?"

"I think we should drop this conversation. It's old hat. Just give him a call. Vince and I talk often about how much we always had fun with you two. It will be like old times."

Once Jane and Marie finished their conversation, Jane called Nick. He looked at the screen and debated whether to answer. It rang a few times and she was getting ready to leave a message when he picked up the telephone. "Hello, Jane."

"Hi, Nick. I'm calling to let you know that Vince and Marie will be coming to town this weekend; and I invited them for a cookout at my home next Sunday afternoon. Would you be interested in coming over? They are excited to see you and are anxious to relive old times."

"I would love to go back to old times, Jane. The current times aren't very much fun."

Jane ignored that response and said, "Would you consider coming over, say around 1:00 Sunday? We could spend the afternoon together and have some serious discussion. I guess I should ask first where you are presently. With cell phones, one person could be in Ohio and the other in Italy."

"Actually, I'm at my home in Florida so no problem getting there Sunday. And what would we talk about, Jane? How you don't want a serious relationship; or would it be no commitments, no attachments; or would it be 'I love you, Nick, but don't want it to go any further?'"

"Why do we always have these types of conversations, Nick? Just come over at 1:00 and I promise to be very honest and talk openly and reasonably."

"I haven't heard those words for a long time so guess it won't hurt. Do you want me to bring anything?"

"A bottle of your good Italian wine would be nice."

"That will work. See you Sunday." Then Nick hung up with no goodbyes or I love you.

Jane spent the next few days walking, meditating, and talking to herself. She even talked to God and asked him what to do. It was like he was saying, "What are you so afraid of, Jane? The man worships you. Go to him and ask his forgiveness for your vacillating with his feelings over the years. You are afraid of his hurting you when all the while you are breaking his heart and toying with his love. You are wearing him down, Jane. You can still have your freedom and independence. Just bite the bullet and give in to his love."

Marie and Vince arrived Saturday afternoon and Jane greeted them at the door. "So great to see you two again. Please come in." They hugged and then Jane told Vince to put their luggage in the guest room. Jane and Marie went out to the deck. When Vince came back, they chatted about old times.

13

Later that evening, Marie and Vince went to bed while Jane enjoyed the quiet time alone.

Marie and Vince left early Sunday to go to church with her sister. "We'll be back by 3:00, Jane. Is that okay?"

"Sure. I talked to Nick and he will be arriving about 1:00. There are some things I need to tell him so that will work out perfectly."

Nick came over that Sunday afternoon and Jane ran to him with open arms. She planted a huge kiss on his lips. He didn't respond to the kiss and pulled back. She looked up at him and said quietly, "It's so good to see you, Nick."

"Wow, what brought this on?"

"It's a beautiful day. Let's go out on the deck and let me talk to you. I've been doing a lot of thinking and I've come to a decision."

"Well, we've had these types of discussions in the past, but I'll be open minded and listen to what you have to say."

"They went out on the deck and Jane explained how she had been meditating the past few days and came to the decision that it was her that had been such an ass over the years. "I'm so sorry, Nick. I really do love you with all my heart. If you'll have me, I want to be your wife and spend the rest of my life with you."

"I don't know what to say. Did you just propose to me?"

"I guess that's what I did. Will you please say yes?"

"YES, YES, YES. Ohhh, my God, Jane. I want to run out in the streets and shout it from the rooftops. In fact, I will." Nick then ran out to the street and started screaming, "Jane just asked me to marry her and I said yes. I'm the happiest man alive." The neighbors started coming out of their homes to see what the commotion was all about. The next door neighbor had been close to them over the years and asked, "Nick, are you all right?"

Nick responded, "I can't begin to tell you what a wonderful feeling I have inside of me. It's like a heavy burden has been lifted off my heart. The love of my life has just proposed to me and I said, yes. A miracle has occurred. THANK YOU, GOD!"

The neighbor was so excited and congratulated Nick on finally getting the girl of his dreams.

Nick went back in the house and picked Jane up in his arms. He hugged her so tight she started squirming. "Okay, Nick."

Nick said, "I don't know what to do. I feel like a school boy who just had his first kiss. I am ecstatic with joy."

"Man, I had no idea how much I've hurt you over the years. I feel so guilty and promise to make it up to you. How about I say I love you at least ten times a day. Will that be a good penitence?"

"That's not necessary, but it would be great to hear. I won't demand any suffering on your part. Just don't ever treat me like a bag of trash. That's how I've felt many times over the years. Enough of this negative talk after such an incredible miracle. Let's go upstairs and consummate this miracle."

After a couple of hours making love, they went downstairs to start preparing for the barbeque. As they entered the kitchen, the doorbell rang. "That must be Vince and Marie," said Jane. "We cut that one close."

"We sure did," was Nick's response as he was walking to the door shouting, "Jane proposed to me! Jane proposed to me!" Vince and Marie were standing outside wondering what he was shouting. As he opened the door, he hugged them and said, "Jane proposed to me and I said yes. Isn't it a miracle?"

Marie went in the house to hug Jane. The men stayed in the foyer and Vince said, "It's about time you two tied the knot. So, when is the wedding?"

"Oh my. I've been on cloud nine all afternoon that I didn't even think of that. I had better do it soon before she changes her mind and reverts back to her old self.

It's so good to see you, Vince. Jane told me that you're going on another business trip. Do we have time later to go have a drink and catch up on each other's lives?"

"I have an important business meeting in New York City tomorrow at 3:00PM; then I'm off to Japan and China."

"Man, that's a heavy schedule. I want you to be my best man. Okay?"

"Of course, but the wedding would have to wait at least two-three months since the ladies are going on another trip."

"I've been so ecstatic that I wasn't aware they were planning a trip."

"It came up pretty suddenly. Marie will keep Jane so busy with planning the wedding that I don't think you need to worry about her backing out. Just buy her a big rock for her finger very soon. That will remind her of her promise to you."

"Good idea. Instead of going for that drink, how about going with me now to the jewelry store?"

"Sure, but knowing you, they won't have anything big enough. You'll probably have to have it specially designed and made. Let's just find something temporary until you get want you want."

They went to the kitchen and said they needed to go buy some wine.

Jane said, "But darling, you just brought a bottle of wine. It's right here."

Nick said, "Vince, she just called me darling. I sure hope this isn't a dream and I'm going to wake up in my bed in a few minutes. Will you pinch me?"

"Sure." He pinched Nick so hard that he yelled.

"You didn't have to go to extremes!"

"I know, but it was fun. So, do you feel that you are still dreaming?"

"No. Now I feel like I've died and gone to heaven. We'll see you gals in a little bit. Do you need anything while we're out and about?"

Jane answered, "No, but don't take too long or it will be too dark for us to broil outside."

"Look at that, Vince. There she is, bossing me around like we're already married. Lord only knows how long it will take for me to come down from cloud nine."

The girls just laughed and continued their talking while the guys left on their mission. Since Nick had flown in from Florida, he had a rental car and so did Vince. There they were, standing in the driveway, debating who should drive. Nick said, "I am probably more familiar with this area than you. How about I drive?"

"Sounds good to me."

They went to an independently owned jewelry store and went inside. Nick asked, "What do you have in your most expensive engagement rings?" Three clerks came running but the longest employed one managed to direct the guys to the store's private collection. They were shown five rings and Nick narrowed it down to two. "Vince, which one do you think Jane would like?"

"Well, do you still plan on having one especially designed for her or are you going to have one of these as the permanent one?"

"Knowing Jane, she won't wear something huge and ostentatious; and these two are quite beautiful." Nick looked at the clerk and said, "Can you tell me the quality of the four "Cs?"

The clerk responded, "I'm impressed that you know about color, cut, clarity, and carat. I'll pull the data of these two out of the file. That should help you determine which one you want."

While the clerk was gone, Nick and Vince looked again at all of the collection.

Nick said, "I hadn't planned on buying on impulse but I still like these two. They both really sparkle which tells me that they are pretty exquisite."

The clerk returned with the information and Nick decided to buy the best quality one. They left the store with Nick feeling proud of his purchase.

When they returned to Jane's home, they found the girls out on the deck drinking wine and really enjoying themselves. Nick walked up to Jane, got down one knee and said, "I hope I don't wake up from this dream. Jane you've made me very happy, fulfilled and proud to be your roommate."

As he was taking the ring box out of his pocket, he said, "Will you make my dream come true and be my wife?"

Jane started crying, held out her left hand and said, "Are you nuts?? Why would I do that? I'm kidding. Of course I'll marry you."

"What are you trying to do? Give this old man a heart attack???"

"Sorry, Nick, I just couldn't resist."

The four of them enjoyed the beautiful evening out on the deck. The guys grilled steaks while the ladies went to the kitchen for the rest of the food and wine.

When the ladies came back, they handed the wine to the guys. Nick put the steaks on each plate at the patio table. Everyone sat down and enjoyed the delicious food. While eating, Jane asked Vince how long he would be gone on his trip and he responded 2-3 weeks. Nick said, "I'm also leaving tomorrow for Switzerland. What time does your plane leave?"

"11:30AM."

"Mine's at 10:00. Maybe we can get together at the airport."

"We can try, but you know international flying takes more time for checking in."

Jane interrupted, "I didn't know you were also going on a business trip, Nick. Let's just enjoy this evening and worry about the morning tomorrow."

Nick responded, "There she goes again bossing me around. I love it!"

Vince whispered to Marie, "That won't last long."

Nick said, "We need to stay in touch and plan what we want to do for the auspicious wedding occasion."

Everyone worked at taking things back to the kitchen and putting things away. Then they all headed to bed.

The next morning, as Nick was getting ready to leave, Jane asked him why he hadn't mentioned the business trip when she called him.

"At that moment, I was still unsure of you and didn't see the need. Later, we were enjoying ourselves so much, that I didn't want to ruin the mood. It's been planned for a while. I'll be back in two-three weeks. I promise." He then kissed her so hard. It was almost like an omen.

"Nick, it's okay. I'm not going to change my mind about the proposal. I promise."

"Okay, but I still feel like it's a dream and I'll wake up with our old way of your feelings about commitment." With that being said, Nick kissed Jane again but softly on the cheek and left.

Marie and Vince came down the stairs a few minutes later and he thanked Jane for the wonderful evening. She wished him a safe trip and then went to the kitchen. Vince gave Marie a kiss. "I love you, Marie. You two ladies be safe on your journey. "Yes, dear," was her reply. Then it was Vince's turn to leave for the airport.

The ladies spent the rest of the morning cleaning up from dinner and then catching up on each other's gossip. Jane said, "I forgot how much fun the four of us always had together. We are so blessed to have such wonderful companions. Don't you agree, Marie?"

"I certainly do. I have made some new friends in New Mexico, but nothing like we have, Jane. I'm also so glad to witness your engagement. That's quite some ring you have on your finger. Our next trip will be down memory lane. There is so much to see and do in this beautiful country; and we have just touched the surface over the years."

Jane asked, "We have been so busy that I never asked how your visit went with your sister and how she is doing."

Marie responded, "She looks good. She said that she has appreciated your visits with her as she knows your busy schedule. I also chatted with her doctor to make sure she was telling me everything. He said that she is in pain a lot from the arthritis, but other than that, her health is pretty good. I do feel better now that I've seen her. Now, let's finish up here and go check out our rig. We need to prepare it for our next trip so we can get on the road again."

Chapter Four

O nce the ladies arrived at the dealership, they found their RV at the rear of the property. They were relieved to see that no varmints had done any damage over the months of storage nor was it very dirty.

They made a list of items needed for their travels and then headed for the dealership store to purchase them.

Once they put away their purchases in the rig, they left the dealership in their nice 4X4 super duty diesel truck. Then Jane took Marie over to her sister's to spend some time with her.

That Wednesday afternoon, Jane went after Marie and they headed back to the dealership. Jane backed up to the rig and hooked up on the first try. Marie removed the blocks, hooked up the safety cord and plugged in the lights. "I guess you haven't lost your touch, Jane, of hooking up the rig on the first try."

"If the ground is smooth, it's usually a breeze. Marie, go to the back of the rig and I'll test the lights and brakes."

Marie walked to the rear and told Jane that everything was working properly. As she came back to the truck, she said, "You always got yourself worked up, Jane, over the hooking and unhooking. I thought you got over that lack of confidence."

"It still worries me but I guess that's just my character."

They brought the rig back to Jane's home and loaded up the balance of things that they needed for the trip. They finished their chores by early evening and decided that it was too late to cook anything for dinner. "How about I just prepare a fruit and cheese plate, Marie?"

"That sounds perfect, Jane. I'll get the wine glasses, but let's not get too carried away. I want to be on the road by 7:00 AM."

"That's exactly what I was going to suggest. We can stop at a fast-food restaurant and eat breakfast on the road."

"That sounds like a plan. I'm anxious to get going. It's been far too long since we've been on the road. From the looks of the itinerary that you devised, we have long drives until we reach Wyoming so we had better get a good night's sleep."

As they started to go upstairs to bed, Jane's cell phone rang. It was Nick, saying, "I'm in Switzerland but just wanted to say I love you. I don't know when I'll be back, but I'll keep in touch. By the way, how does that beautiful ring fit on your finger? Does it need to be resized?"

"Actually, you did a pretty good job. I guess you know my body better than I do."

"I guess I've explored it enough over the years. If you have any trouble at all, just go to the jeweler. I left their business card on your counter in the kitchen. I love you so much, Jane. You'll never know how happy you've made me. Sweet dreams, sweetheart."

"You have sweet dreams too, Nick. Please be careful wherever you're going. By the way, where are you going?"

"I have many stops throughout Western Europe. Please don't worry about me. You just take special care on your travels."

After Nick hung up, Jane said, "Well, both of our men are traveling. We need to pray for both of them. Now, let's try and get some sleep. Goodnight, Marie."

Jane was up at 5:30 the next morning and woke up, Marie. "I've put some towels and a wash cloth in the guest bathroom for you. I already took my shower and will work at getting what last-minute things we need. I know that once we leave, your motto is, "If we don't have it, we don't need it."

"That's right, Jane."

"Well, that theory goes with your saying if we can get into a space, we can get out of it; and I tell you that theory doesn't always work. Sometimes when one puts a big rig into a space without first analyzing how to get out, they are stuck in that space. As we've discovered over the years, there were many times that it was fortunate for us to first figure out if we can get out."

"Whatever, Jane. Let me wake up first before you start lecturing. Okay?"

"Sorry!" Jane went into the kitchen and loaded up the two coolers with food from the refrigerator and freezer. She took them out to the rig and stocked the refrigerator. She then went back in the house and grabbed her clothes.

Marie had finished getting dressed and packed her last-minute clothes and toiletries. She came downstairs and took her things out to the rig. When she went back in the house, she saw Jane coming down the stairs, "Is there anything I can help you with?"

"Please get the list that's on the counter in the kitchen. We need to make sure we have everything. You can read each thing on the list and check it off as I find it."

Marie said, "Now why does it not surprise me that you made a list!"

"Just read, okay?"

"Okay!"

Once that task was completed, Jane walked through the house and took one last look to make sure it was secured. "Let's go, Marie."

As they walked out of the house, Jane locked the door and they went back out to the rig. Marie removed the blocks from behind the wheels while Jane started the engine in the truck. Marie made sure everything was secured in the rig and then also got in the truck. She took out the log book and asked Jane what was on the odometer and marked it down. Jane asked, "Are we set to go?"

"All set, captain. It 6:50AM and we are off on another adventure."

Chapter Five

The ladies traveled for about one hour before they saw a fast-food restaurant. Jane said, "Let's just pick up something and eat on the road. We have a lot of miles to cover. I'll just pull up to the right side of the restaurant and park in that long lane. That way I can swing around the restaurant on the way out."

"That's fine with me, Jane. I'll go in and order for us. I'm going to get a large decaf black coffee and an egg and cheese sandwich. What would you like?"

"Funny, as that's what I was thinking of ordering. That will make it simple."

Once Jane had the rig parked, Marie went into the restaurant and ordered their food. She wasn't gone very long and they managed to get back out on the highway with no trouble.

Marie said, "I see that you haven't forgotten how to manage this big rig, Jane. You are a natural."

"I don't know about that, but I do feel comfortable driving this thing. However, I don't think I'll ever master that backing up, no matter how much I practice."

"We've always managed without it, Jane. Those truck drivers pulling two and three trailers can't back up either, so don't let it get you down."

Jane said, "Enough talk on that subject. I was going to make Rock Island, Illinois our first stop, but it's 525 miles. Let's stop in South Bend, Indiana overnight and then head to Rock Island. Do you mind if we don't unhook the truck from the rig?"

"Not at all; but we haven't even made our first campground and you're already changing plans. Poor Timmy, our GPS, is always confused by you."

"Well, that's the joy of traveling via RV. You can always change your mind."

They arrived at the campground by early afternoon and it even had pull throughs. They found a site with a patio and Jane managed to get into their space without incident.

Marie got out of the truck and put the blocks behind the wheels and hooked up the water and electric. Jane performed her arrival duties; and commented that she was getting hungry.

"That must be why my stomach is growling. Let's go inside and fix lunch."

After lunch, the ladies got their lounge chairs from the storage compartment and sat down by the side of the rig. "I have really missed doing this, Marie. We each enjoy our sweethearts, but this is so much fun. We are so blessed."

"We certainly are blessed. After many years of being single, I've been in seventh heaven. Vince is so good to me, but he travels a lot and it gets pretty lonely in that huge hacienda up in the foothills of New Mexico."

While they were reading their books, the wind started to blow and then dark clouds started to appear.

Jane said, "It looks like we aren't going to be able to do this very long. I think we should go look for twigs just in case we can build a fire later."

"Okay, but let's not get too much as we have to leave tomorrow and I don't want to store wood."

By the time the ladies found their twigs, the wind was really blowing. They returned to the rig just in time as it started to sprinkle and then came the downpour. They spent the rest of the afternoon and evening relaxing and watching a movie.

"What do you want to have for dinner, Marie?"

"Since we had a late lunch, I'm really not that hungry. Let's just make a salad."

"Okay. I'll set the table while you get all of the fixins out of the refrigerator."

"Fixins, Jane? What are fixins?"

"Very funny!"

By the time they ate dinner and cleaned everything, the storm had stopped so they went back outside and started a fire in the fire ring. Jane said, "This was a wonderful day. I'm so glad that you like to do this, Marie; and I really appreciate Vince allowing you to go on this adventure."

"Vince didn't ALLOW me to do this. We have a wonderful marriage and let each other have our freedom to do as we wish without permission or approval. Yes, we discuss things together, but we are independent of each other and it works very well."

Jane said, "I guess Nick and I also have the same arrangement. For years I was so worried about losing my independence if I made a commitment; but seeing you two so happy helped me make my decision to propose to Nick. I have to admit that I really feel relieved and at peace with myself. I guess I should have made this decision years ago."

"That's what we three kept trying to tell you; and we are so glad that you finally came to your senses. It's getting late. Let's put out the fire and get to bed. We still have a long way to go before we can really relax."

Chapter Six

The next morning the ladies prepared for departure and were on the road by 8:00AM. They traveled through the rest of Indiana and stopped in Morris, Illinois for lunch. As they were driving through town, they found a quaint small restaurant with a large parking lot. Marie said, "This must be a good stop for the truckers since this small restaurant has such large parking."

"Well, the owners could also own the adjacent land and don't want any other restaurants next to them."

"There goes your real estate background again, Jane, but you're probably accurate on that statement. Go ahead and pull in with your pull-through expertise!"

"Very funny snide remark, Marie."

"Just making a switch and pulling your chain for once."

Once inside, they quickly found a table and ordered. While waiting for the food, Jane said, "We're making good time so far."

"Yes we are and that's a good thing. I'm looking at the itinerary and today is the longest run at 330 miles so we had better eat fast and get back on the road."

"Eye eye, Captain."

"As if I'm the one in charge—HAH HAH!"

Fortunately, the gals were having good weather and made it to their next stop in Rock Island, Illinois by late afternoon. They once again stayed attached to the RV and hooked up the water, sewer, and electric. Jane worked on plugging in the cable for the television while Marie set up the chairs and readied the campfire. "Let's just have sandwiches for dinner, Jane. I'm too tired to prepare a meal and do dishes."

"I couldn't agree more. We still have 275 miles to travel tomorrow, but I have us staying at the next campground until Monday."

"I'm glad as I need a rest from that truck."

"You should be behind the wheel driving that big truck and pulling our house behind it."

"I'm sorry, Jane. I really appreciate your driving, as my eyesight isn't what it used to be. You're doing a fine job being my chauffeur. I was just making a comment."

"That's okay, Marie. I guess I'm just tired. We're already pushing ourselves too hard. The next three days will be relaxing. The campground directory says there's a Strategic Air & Space Museum to tour. We could also see Boys Town."

"While that all sounds thrilling, let's play it by ear."

Jane's cell phone rang and it was Nick. "I'm in Lake Lucerne, Switzerland and it's absolutely breathtaking. I wish you were here. Maybe we can come here for our honeymoon."

"That sounds like a plan. I really haven't thought about places for the honeymoon as I'm trying to concentrate first on the wedding."

"That surely is wonderful news as I keep worrying that you'll change your mind."

"Remember, I'm the one that proposed to you so I'm committed. Imagine me using that word! On another note, how are the business meetings going?"

"This is my second stop of the itinerary. Tonight I'm heading for Paris. I'll be in that area for a few days and then head for home. So far this is a very successful trip. I might even make enough money to break even on that rock that's on your finger."

"This rock is beautiful, but I would have settled for a cigar band."

"Sure you would! I love you, Jane. Please drive carefully. By the way, where are you two now?"

"We're in Rock Island, Illinois and heading for Omaha, Nebraska tomorrow."

"As I said, be careful. I love you very much, Jane."

"Ditto."

"That's all I get? Ditto??"

"All right. I love you Nicholas Camboli—I love you—I love you—I love you!"

"That's better. Goodnight my love."

Chapter Seven

Friday the ladies traveled across Iowa and made it to Omaha, Nebraska by early afternoon. As they pulled into the campground, they saw all kinds of things that they could do over their three-day weekend, including shuffleboard, mini golf, swimming, and even badminton.

When they entered the camp store to register, Jane asked if they had pull-through sites. "Of course," said the manager. "You will be pleased as the pads are concrete and we've provided nice patio furniture. You'll even see a Chiminea at your site."

Marie whispered to Jane, "What's a Chiminea?" The manager heard Jane and responded, "It's a place to burn your firewood." Marie's face turned beet red. As they walked out Marie said, "How embarrassing!"

Jane said, "Don't fret, Marie. You're very intelligent and always using words that I have no idea what they mean."

They found their site and Jane pulled in with no difficulty. "This is really wonderful, Marie. The truck should unhook from the 5th wheel with no difficulty since we're on a concrete pad."

"That's good as I know you always worry about the challenges of unhooking and hooking up. When we were originally looking at ways to travel, we knew this could be an issue, but decided that we didn't want to pull a car behind those large motor homes."

The ladies proceeded to perform their arrival duties and were in their chairs outside under the awning by 3:00. "It took us a few days, but we can now relax for the weekend," said Jane.

"Yes, we can even see the lake over there. This is surely a beautiful site. I'm going in and fix myself a cocktail. Would you like one?"

"After driving a total of about 830 miles over these past few days, I'm definitely ready for one, thank you."

While Marie was inside fixing the cocktails, Jane worked at preparing a fire in their fancy fire pit. Once she finished that chore, she got the charcoal grill out of storage and attached it at the rear of the rig. She had to crawl underneath the rig to attach the gas hose. That was quite a challenge, lying on her back on the ground. She tried pushing, then twisting, then pulling. After a few swear words and struggling, she finally had it secured.

She walked back to the storage compartment and pulled out the portable lounge chairs. As she was walking back to the patio to set them up, Marie came out with the drinks. She had also prepared a pu-pu platter. "I wondered what was taking you so long, Marie."

"Well, I see you've also been busy while I was inside."

"Since we haven't had a decent evening meal yet, I thought we would grill steaks and have our fancy potatoes with grilled onions and garlic."

"That sounds yummy, Jane, but let's wait a while. I want to just sit here, enjoy the beautiful afternoon and just relax."

"I second that! By the way, I know I gripe about it every time I hook it up, but the manufacturer of this rig did a crappy job of engineering when he/she decided to put the grill gas valve UNDER the rig. You need to be a contortionist to hook the nozzle to it."

"Yes, you do gripe about it every time, but that's okay. It is what it is. There's nothing we can do about it, unless we sell the rig and get another one."

"FINE, I said my peace so let's just relax and read our books. Nice appetizers, by the way. They hit the spot."

Saturday the ladies went for a long walk around the campground in the morning and found some kindling for their evening fire. They played some badminton and enjoyed a swim in the afternoon. They made a salad for dinner and then drove around Omaha in the evening.

Sunday morning they attended church and then toured the Strategic Air & Space Museum. "We really have found some nice museums in our travels, haven't we Jane."

"We sure have and this one ranks right up there with the rest of them."

Once the ladies returned to their campsite, they relaxed around the fire. Vince called Marie and said his business trip was going smoothly. "It's nice that Vince called you, Marie. I've been concerned that Nick hasn't called. The other night, he said he would update me every evening."

"I'm sure he's just been too occupied with work; and you know how exhausting that traveling can be, going from place to place. The packing and unpacking plus getting boarding passes, checking luggage, etc. You always commented how your staff would say, "have fun" whenever you had business trips. They always schedule conferences in touristy places and one never has time to enjoy them when you're sitting in meetings from morning to night."

As they were talking, Jane's cell phone rang. Jane said, speak of the devil, thinking it was Nick. It was Nick's sister. She didn't know how to tell Jane gently so just said, "You probably know that Nick was on a business trip to Western Europe. There was a bad storm that surfaced while the plane was in the air. The pilot called in a mayday saying they were over the Alps and then the tower received no further communication. It appears that the tower lost the signal. This all happened yesterday and there has been no further communication. I'm sorry to tell you this over the telephone, but wanted you to know before you heard it on the news."

Jane just went numb and dropped the telephone. She was white as a sheet and Marie shouted, "Jane, what's wrong?" Jane didn't answer so Marie picked up Jane's phone and asked, "Who is this?" Nick's sister proceeded to explain it again to Marie. Marie gave Nick's sister her cell phone number and asked her to please call with any updates. Marie then hugged Jane and continued to comfort her.

Jane said, "I know Nick is all right. He is a survivor. If the plane did go down, I'm sure he is tending to all of the passengers. I will be hearing from him shortly."

"You are probably right, Jane. Let's call Vince as he has friends in high places at the FAA. You can fill him in on what Nick told you about his location last Thursday and where he was heading Friday."

Marie called Vince and told him what had happened. She then gave Jane the telephone so Jane could give him the details. Vince told Jane that he had some friends high up in the FAA. He would contact them to see what they knew and get back to her.

The ladies put out their fire in the fire pit, put away their chairs and went inside. Jane turned on the television to see what the news had to report. It really said no more than Jane already knew.

Marie said, "We can wait until Tuesday to travel if it would make you feel more comfortable, Jane."

"Not really. I'm the type that handles things better if I keep busy. It helps to keep the worrying at bay. We're heading to Gothenburg, Nebraska tomorrow, which is about 265 miles away. Let's try and get some sleep." Needless to say, Jane didn't sleep much that night.

Chapter Eight

Somewhere high in the Alps Nick's plane had crashed. There were over 100 people on board, including the pilot and crew. The pilot had been having trouble navigating due to a terrible storm. He reported to all passengers that there would be turbulence and to fasten their seat belts. The further they flew, the worse the storm got so the pilot relayed a mayday to the closest tower. Shortly thereafter, he had no communication. The pilot decided to try and land wherever possible. The plane was going very slow and suddenly it crashed into the side of a mountain. The front half of the plane hit hard and the back half hit the ground. All of the crew and most of the passengers did not survive.

Nick fortunately was in the back part of the plane when it hit. He was still strapped in his seat and had a large piece of the plane lying on top of him. He unbuckled the seat belt and tried pushing the piece away from him. It was a struggle but he finally managed to get out from under it. He started to stand up. That's when he noticed that his left leg felt very strange and had sharp shooting pains. He checked it and saw no blood so he started walking through the mangled mess. With all of the debris and bodies lying around, it was difficult to find a clear path to walk. The leg was so painful that he sat back down and massaged it for a while. That was also challenging as his left hand was bent really bad. Then he saw a lady checking passengers and asked if she was a doctor.

"No, but I'm a registered nurse. I was on my way back to Paris. I had attended a medical conference in Lucerne so fortunately, I have a lot of medical supplies. From looking at your left hand, I can see that you need my services."

"I was sitting in a window seat when we crashed and the wall crushed my left side. I also think there's something serious going on with my left leg. If you have some happy pills in your medical supplies, we'll worry about the leg later and concentrate on those that survived."

She reset Nick's hand and put it in a sling. He wasn't too happy about that as he knew it would be very awkward to address the many tasks at hand. Then she asked, "Do you have any medical skills?"

"I had combat training while in the service and tended to a lot of the wounded. Would that classify as medical skills?"

"It'll have to do. By the way, my name is Melina."

"Glad to meet you, Melina, and wish it was under better circumstances. My name is Nick. I think the first order of business is to check and see who survived. By the way, you don't look so good yourself."

"Boy, you're really good with the compliments. I also was in a window seat and was stuck under parts of the plane. I managed to push them away. I have a serious gash on my right thigh so found a turnicate. I also popped my right shoulder back into place and have some broken ribs. Other than that I have scrapes and bruises. I've been tagging those that didn't make it. So far, I found four others that are alive. Two are barely making it and I don't think that I can help either of them. The other two keep drifting in and out of consciousness."

"How can I help?"

"I can really use some hot water and towels."

"And I could use a hot juicy steak to eat, but we all can't have everything that we want."

"You keep surprising me with your witty comments. Can you at least find water?"

"That I can do. If nothing else, I can melt the snow from outside."

"There should be some clean towels that the flight attendants gave to first-class passengers. See if you can find them and then start cleaning up the passengers. I've been helping this gentleman. He's French and says his name is Jean Claude. He has some broken ribs and a large gash on his back. I can't do anything about the broken ribs, but I'll use the water to clean around the gash. It's pretty deep, but if I can stop the bleeding and use some of my magical supplies, I think he'll be okay."

In his strong French accent, Jean Claude said, "I'm right here. You don't need to talk in the third person; and then he passed out."

The back part of the plane had a food station area and it was pretty damaged. Nick proceeded to move the debris and found some bottled water. In fact, the bottles were all over the place. From his survival days, he managed to get the hot plate working and heated the water. He surprised Melina with her boiled water and some towels that he found.

While Melina was tending to the injured, Nick said, "We're starting to get natural light, which is a good thing. I'll work at boarding up some holes to stop the blizzard that's coming in here. At least I'll give it a try."

"It's nice to be positive, but this place is a disaster. There's no way that you can cover all of these open areas."

"My fiancée always says, "If you don't try, then there's no result."

"Smart fiancée."

Chapter Nine

Jane decided to get up at 5:30 since she hardly slept anyway. She was making coffee when Marie came down to the kitchen area. "Apparently you didn't get much sleep last night, Jane."

"You are correct. I'm so worried about Nick but feel it in my bones that he is alive. Let's pretend that everything is normal and let's try to enjoy our trip."

"It seems that we forgot to have dinner last evening. How about I fix us some scrambled eggs and sausage?"

"You can fix some for yourself. I think I'll just have a piece of toast. My stomach is in a turmoil right now."

The ladies managed to be on the road Monday by 7:00AM and hit some bad weather that morning. While Jane was driving, she asked Marie, "I noticed in the camp directory that we are heading for Grand Island, Nebraska. It's probably about another 80 miles. Would you mind calling the KOA campground and ask if they have any pull-through sites available? I really am in no mood to wrestle with this weather. We can just spend the night and head for Gothenburg tomorrow. That was going to be about 265 miles anyway, so it will help shorten the ride tomorrow."

"Of course I'll do that Jane. I'm not too keen on riding in this stuff either; and shortening the ride tomorrow is music to my ears." She called and they did have a site available. The ladies made it there by noon.

After they were all settled, Marie said, "Boy, that was a good decision as this weather is getting worse!" Marie's cell phone rang and it was Vince. She answered and said, "Hi honey, do you have good news for us?" As he started reporting to her, she stopped him and asked if she could put the phone on speaker so Jane could also hear the update. He said that was perfectly fine.

"They've sent rescue teams up to the mountain area near the town of Bern, Switzerland. Apparently the plane had just taken off and wasn't in the air very long when the pilot reported the mayday. I guess the weather had been bad all day and the tower really shouldn't have let them go."

Jane said, "Well, that's just special! I have lots of questions and you may not be able to answer them. Do you know if the storm has subsided; how many search teams are there; who do they report to and how often; what kind of terrain are they encountering; can I go with them?"

Vince said, "Boy, Jane, you do have lots of questions. Let me get back to you on them."

Marie said, "Jane, you need to remember that Vince is also on a business trip and your inquiries will take some time."

"I'm sorry, Vince. I'm a little on edge and feel helpless."

"That's okay, Jane. I'm presently in Tokyo, Japan and just woke up. I can't meet with my partners until tomorrow, so I have all day today to work on this. Remember, though, that I'm 13 hours ahead of you so it's presently 4:30AM Tuesday here in Tokyo."

"I really appreciate your efforts, Vince. I finally made a commitment to my sweetheart and then lost him again."

"You didn't lose him, Jane. He's my best friend so I have a stake in this also. I know it's easy to say, but try and keep calm and have patience. There are professionals working on that mountain and they will find him. Have faith. Marie, can you go off speaker now?"

Marie took the phone off speaker and said, "I miss you terribly Vince. Jane is a basket case, but tries to make this trip as normal as possible. She really does appreciate your help. Please remember to keep yourself safe. We don't need both of our men lost in the masses."

"I'm fine, Marie. I'll keep in touch. Love you, sweetheart. Goodbye."

Jane spent the rest of the afternoon catching up with writing in their journal. Marie decided to bake a cake and do the weekly cleaning.

When she finished baking, she let it cool and then cut a piece for each of them. Jane said, "This cake is really delicious. I'm not one for cake, but this is really moist. You didn't spend much time making it and I noticed that you didn't even use the mixer. An old friend gave me a recipe similar to this years ago. It's just oatmeal, flour, butter, eggs, and cocoa."

"That's basically what I used. I also mixed some semi-sweet chocolate in the batter. Once in the pan, I sprinkled some on top so there's no frosting. Very simple to make and very delicious but that's the problem. It's so good that I want to eat half of it in one sitting."

"Not if I beat you to it!"

That evening they watched the news. It had nothing to report other than to say that rescue men and women had flown in from all over Europe. The teams had made it halfway up the summit and the weather had subsided, but they hadn't found any evidence of the plane.

Jane said, "From the looks of the terrain, those rescue teams must have had a lot of training dealing with bad weather, climbing over boulders, and even rappelling. I don't think I would want that job. In fact, I know that I wouldn't want that job."

"I guess there's a skill set for everyone, Jane."

"That's for sure. Many people ask me why I love my job as the owners aren't happy when I spend too much of their money to keep the tenants happy; but the tenants aren't happy because they want more amenities in the building which means I would spend lots of the owner's money."

"I also get comments about how I can have the patience and understanding of children versus their parents. I have to place allegedly abused children in children's services facilities until the courts can decide if the parents actually committed an abused deed. Many times the children are so messed up that our social services department wonders if the children will ever be able to lead normal lives again."

"We surely are blessed, Marie, to have the freedom we have and enjoy our amazing mates. I keep praying that Nick is okay and will come back to me."

"He will come back to you, Jane. Like Vince says, you need to have faith and patience."

"The storm has subsided. Let's go for a walk around the campground and get rid of some of these calories that we just took into our bodies."

Chapter Ten

Tuesday, the ladies made it to Gothenburg, Nebraska safely and the weather was very good to them. They were settled in and unhooked easily at their campsite. "Since we lost a day due to weather, we may want to spend an extra day here before heading to Wyoming, Marie."

"Why's that?"

"Well, the directory says the campground owners are from England. It would be fascinating to chat with them for awhile. Then there's hiking trails along the South Platte River. I guess there are many beaver dams along the river. That would be interesting to see. We may also want to investigate the Golden Spike Tower."

"What the hell is that?"

WOW—some foul mouth the lady has."

"Just answer the question."

"I have no idea. That's why I said we need to investigate."

"So glad to see you're feeling more at ease, Jane."

"The worry is still there, but I want to make this trip fun; and I certainly don't want to ruin it for you."

"You have enough to worry about without adding me to your list. I'm fine."

Just then Marie's cell phone rang and it was Vince so she put him on speaker phone. "Good morning, ladies. I spent the day yesterday chatting with my friends at the FAA, but they really don't have much to report yet. Let's see if I can answer all of your questions, Jane. Yes, the storm has subsided. It's sunny and should remain that way for a few days. Needless to say, that's something in our favor. If anyone is alive, they should also be blessed with good weather. Sorry I said that. We all know that Nick is alive; there are a total of 30 men and women on search teams. They formed six teams of five each. They spread out over 30 miles and are hiking up the mountain, as we speak. They all have radios and cell phones, but the cell phones are intermittent. The head of each team reports back to the command center in Bern. That's where my contacts are. Also, the media constantly bugs them; the terrain is very rugged but these people have many years of training and experience. Many are mountain guides as their main profession. I don't think I would want that profession but guess there's something for everyone."

The ladies chimed in and told Vince that they had just had that same conversation relating to professions.

"Back to your list, Jane. I believe there was only one more item where you asked if you could go. With my mentioning how rugged it is and the years of training and experiences of the rescue teams, I think you know the answer to that question. Besides, you ladies are on another adventure and I think you would be of more help to Nick by continuing on that adventure."

"You are probably right, Vince. I would just be a handicap to those trying to find the plane. I would even probably set them back a day or two."

Vince replied, "I don't know if it would set them back, but you definitely would not be of any help."

"Thank you, buddy. That makes me feel better—HAH!"

"Sorry, just being honest. I love you, Mrs. Lechendyke. It's 6:30AM here and I have meetings all day starting at 8:00AM so had better get busy so I can earn money to keep my sweetheart in the manner to which she is accustomed."

"Thank you Mr. Lechendyke. I appreciate that. Just keep safe and come back to me."

"Yes my sweet. Have a great day you two. Goodbye."

Jane said, "I'm feeling better knowing that the weather will be good and those rescue workers had better get their butts in gear and find my sweetheart. Now, let's go chat with those English folk, Marie."

"I thought you'd never ask."

They walked up to the camping store and found the English couple sitting in a circle chatting with other campers. They joined in and listened to the couple telling their fascinating adventures. They had traveled all over the world and they were talking about hiking the Himalayas. Jane chimed in and said, "What a wonderful experience. How many miles did you hike and what was your highest altitude?" The wife stated that they made it to one summit at about 12,000 feet. Jane inquired if they had any breathing problems at that altitude. No, was the answer, "But I developed a slight headache."

As the ladies walked back to their campsite, Marie said, "WOW, did they have experiences or what."

"Well, if you look back at what we've done over the years, we've had some awesome experiences ourselves. There's our local canoe trips; but that one along the Pocomoke River in Maryland canoeing from bed and breakfast to bed and breakfast homes was awesome. Then what about that three week trip we took with Helen all along northern United States and up into Canada to see Lake Louise? I could go on and on."

"You're absolutely right, but still to backpack the Himalayas would be the trip of a lifetime."

"Well, I guess you just have to put it on your bucket list, Marie."

"With these old bones, I have enough trouble walking the flat trails on our trips. Speaking of hiking, let's explore the nature trail, here along the South Platte River."

"Sounds like a plan. We did say that we could leave Friday. That's the beauty of traveling via recreational vehicle. You can do whatever you want and whenever. Besides that nature trail is calling our name."

The next morning the ladies had their breakfast, showered, and were on the trail by 10:00AM. They found a log cabin that had been a Pony Express Station in its day. Then they crossed the river and saw a 4' waterfall. "Be careful, Marie. This area is very slippery."

"Don't baby me, Jane. I'm not that old."

"I know, but you have a tendency to fall on occasion and this would not be a good spot to do that."

"Is there ever a good place to fall?"

"Good point."

Further up the trail they saw some canoeists along the river.

"My goodness, Marie. There's our passion. Let's find time to do that."

"Let's go back to the camping store and find out where we can rent a canoe. We can't go far as we probably wouldn't be on the river before 1:00. We didn't see any Beaver Dam so maybe we can find one while canoeing."

As the ladies were hiking back to their campsite, Marie tripped on a stone and fell. When she tried to get up, she fell again. "I'm so sorry, Jane. Your clumsy hiking friend can't seem to ever make it through a trip without breaking something."

"Why do you think you broke something?"

"Well, I can't seem to put any pressure on my left foot."

Just then, two men came up the trail and saw the ladies. One of them said, "Are you ladies okay?"

Jane responded that her friend had tripped and can't seem to put any pressure on her left foot.

"I'm a doctor." As he was looking at Marie, he said, "Do you mind if I look at it mam?"

"If you don't mind; and please call me Marie." Marie pointed to the campground and said, "We're staying at that campground over there and I would like to try and get back there."

"Well, to accomplish that, you have two choices. I can carry you to your campsite or you can wait here while I go to my car and get some supplies.

"Waiting is my preference, if that works for you."

He chuckled and said, "Believe it or not, I was going to deliver some crutches to a friend after my hike. You are welcome to have them. However, after looking at your foot, I don't think it is broken, but highly advise getting it x-rayed. There is a medical center in Gothenburg. I can give you the address."

"Thank you, sir. What is your name?"

"Frank Slischburg, MD at your service mam, I mean Marie. You may use my name at the medical center, if you like. In fact, I have the day off but am willing to meet you there, say at 3:00?"

Marie looked at Jane and she nodded yes, So Marie said, "Sure."

The two men left and Jane pulled out a blanket from her backpack and put it down alongside the trail. "Can you scoot yourself over to the blanket, Marie? There are more people coming along the trail and I don't want them walking over you."

"I hardly think that would happen but, yes, I can scoot over."

"Are you in any pain?"

"Just discomfort and bruised ego."

"It can happen to anyone."

"But it never happens to you, Jane. Only clumsy me."

Jane found some water in her backpack. She sat down next to Marie and waited for the men to come back. "That doctor is pretty good looking, Marie."

"Better than Nick?"

"No one could be better than Nick."

Just then, only Frank came back.

Jane asked, "Where is your friend?"

"We usually meet in the parking lot and hike this trail every morning. We were getting ready to go our separate ways when we bumped into you ladies."

Marie said, "I'm so sorry that I interrupted your hike."

"You didn't interrupt us. We needed to get moving anyway. By the way, I introduced myself, but didn't catch your friend's name, Marie."

Marie said, "How rude of us. This is my friend, Jane."

"Frank had a twinkle in his eye and said, "Glad to meet you, Jane. Sorry it was under these circumstances."

"So am I," responded Marie.

After Frank wrapped Marie's foot, he adjusted the crutches and handed them to her. "Have you ever used crutches?"

Jane responded, "She's a pro at this sort of thing. We travel a lot together and she has a tendency to injure herself in one way or another. I think we've visited a hospital or medical center in just about every state that we've visited."

Marie said, "You don't need to make it sound like I'm falling apart. I admit that I'm clumsy, but I have really bad Osteoporosis."

"Well, ladies. I need to get going. I'll meet you at the medical center at 3:00 today."

Marie said, "Thank you again, Frank. You are a Godsend."

With that, he left.

Jane helped Marie get up. She was folding the blanket when Marie commented, "You didn't need to tell him that I'm the clumsiest woman on earth."

"I didn't say that, but I'm sure he'll see on the x-rays how many fractures you've had over the years."

With that, Marie hobbled along while Jane slowly walked beside her as they headed back to the campsite.

Jane made some lunch and Marie said, "I guess the canoeing is out for the day."

"I think canoeing could probably be out for the rest of the trip. Maybe the x-rays will give us good news. That Frank appears to know his stuff. Hopefully, he can get you fixed in no time at all."

"That's what I like about you. You're always thinking positive."

Chapter Eleven

With Nick's hand in a sling, he was struggling with trying to plug the gaping holes of the plane. He went through the entire carry-on luggage to see if there would be any tools. He knew that was going to be in vain as the TSA would have confiscated them but he looked anyhow. Having found none, he limped back to the attendant's station and managed to find a small hammer and screw driver. His leg was really bothering him so he went back to Melina and sat down.

Melina asked, "Did you find any blankets or coats?"

"As a matter of fact, I did. I'll work on cleaning the blood off those you haven't taken care of yet. Then, I'll put blankets on them and hopefully get them warm. Should I also give them some water?"

"Sure, but do it slowly. With their lying down on the floor, it'll be challenging to get it in their mouths."

"I think I can figure out how to give it to them. How about I hold up their heads??"

"There goes that sarcasm again. Just do it. I'm so glad that I have these supplies. Some are the latest out on the market today, especially the pain killers. God was shining down on us."

"If you say so."

"You don't believe in God?"

"Of course I do but, I don't understand why this had to happen. I've been in a relationship on and off for years. My sweetheart was against commitment and would break up with me many times. Believe it or not, she finally committed. In fact, she just proposed to me ten days ago. Such irony!"

"We will get out of this alive, Nick; and you'll be back in your sweetheart's arms again very soon. Have faith."

After Nick cleaned up the passengers and got them warm, he worked again at trying to plug in the gaping holes of the plane. While he was struggling with a piece, Jean Claude came up to help. "Two hands are better than one, especially since you only have one, Nick."

"Thanks, but are you sure that you should be standing right now? I don't want you passing out on us again."

"I need to get moving and get the blood flowing so I can keep warm and these gaping holes aren't helping the situation."

Once the guys filled what holes they could, they decided next to work on getting some communication. They found many cell phones but most of them were dead. Nick said, "I'll take these outside to see if we can get any reception." As he started to go, he lost his balance. Jean Claude said, "How about I go outside while you work on some of them in here; and I strongly suggest that you sit down and rest that leg of yours."

In a very frustrated tone, Nick said, "Fine!"

The blizzard had stopped and it was a bright sunny Saturday afternoon. The snow was very deep but Jean

Claude managed to walk a few yards with some of the cell phones trying to get reception. Some of the phones were already dead, but he managed to get one to work. He dialed 911 but no response. He messaged a May Day hoping someone would see it. He went back inside to see if Nick had any success. "No," was the answer. Then they saw Melina. She managed to find one of the seats and was just sitting there sobbing.

Jean Claude asked, "What's the matter, Melina?"

"I just lost one of the passengers. We are down to only five of us and one is still unconscious. A lady was heading to visit her daughter in Paris. Her name is Bridgett. She may lose her arm. It also appears that she has a broken neck in three places, causing her to be completely paralyzed. I did the best I could to keep her comfortable. She is resting." Malina whispered to Nick, 'I don't think she's going to make it; and I don't know if I can save the other one.' This is really putting my skills to the test."

Nick said, "You're doing an incredible job. Don't lose confidence in yourself. I need you to be positive and keep us alive until the rescue teams get here; and they will get here. Let's finish up in helping the injured as much as we can. Tomorrow, I think we should concentrate on trying to get some form of communication to the outside world. Maybe we can build a fire."

"Yes, we need some type of communication, but building a fire sounds very improbable. We need to use what wood we have for boarding up some more holes. We may also need it to fend off predators."

"Speaking of helping the injured, let me look at your leg. It doesn't appear to be broken but it's getting more swollen." She wondered if the leg could be saved. She didn't tell him how concerned she was about it.

"So what's the verdict, doctor?"

"I'm no doctor, but I'm concerned about the swelling. I know it won't do any good to say this, but you need to stay off that leg. I can give you medication for the pain, but you really need to be in a hospital."

"Well, since I can't call for an ambulance, let's just pretend that it's fine for now. How about I go back to the attendant's station and get all of us some food."

"Why don't you sit in this chair and I'll go get the food."

Jean Claude was feeling better and chimed in, "I'll help you, Melina."

"You two don't need to treat me like I'm an invalid."

Melina said, "We're just trying to help that leg of yours; so please rest for just a few minutes."

Fortunately, there was a lot of food as the flight attendants hadn't had a chance to serve any of it. Jean Claude brought some food to Nick while Melina fed those that had regained consciousness.

By Monday, they lost Bridgette but the one remaining finally stayed conscious and was getting stronger. He had a deep gash on the top of his head and couldn't remember his name or why he had taken the flight. He started screaming and tried running out of the plane. Jean Claude caught him and Melina gave him a shot to sedate him. Nick cleared an area on the floor and made a haphazard bed and then laid the gentleman down on it.

The weather continued to be sunny but very cold. Fortunately, the wind had died down so they all were comfortable, at least as good as possible considering the circumstances.

Melina said to the guys, "I have a feeling that we're going to be trapped in here for a while so I have an unpleasant suggestion to make, if you can handle the task."

Nick said, "I have a feeling that the task is removing dead bodies."

"And where would you put them?"

"I checked outside earlier and it's a pretty rough terrain but we have no choice. Jean Claude and I will take those that you've tagged. We'll make an area outside and stack them the best that we can. I know that sounds morbid but there's no other choice."

There were many bodies and some of them were pretty mangled. It was a gruesome task and the guys had a hard time trying not to vomit.

After they came back inside, the three of them performed a memorial service for those that had expired. Then they just sat down and were very quiet for a while.

Then Jean Claude asked Nick, "Are you up to taking a hike down the mountain? We need to reach civilization or at least someone who can go and get us some help."

"Sure, I'm fine, but what about you?"

Jean Claude looked at Nick and said, "Let's see, I have broken ribs, which makes it hard to breathe. That's probably not a good thing considering we're probably at least 14,000' in the air. Melina did a good job patching up the hole in my back. Now, there's you with a sling on your arm and that limp isn't going to help as we will probably encounter steep terrain and lots of rocks and boulders. We will also need to figure out how to make snow shoes, as the snow can be 100′ deep."

"WOW—you really know how to encourage a person to go on a hike with you. That was quite some pep talk unless I didn't understand that French-speaking accent."

Melina interrupted the conversation and said, "Are you two nuts??? To begin with, neither one of you is in any shape to go 100′ let alone 2-5 miles down the mountain."

Nick said, "Do you have any other ideas? Jean Claude and I have worked on the cell phones to no avail. We can just stay in here and wait for the rescue teams to find us. At least I'm assuming there are rescue teams looking for us. However, this is a big mountain and we are stuck at the top of civilization."

Jean Claude said, "Before we leave tomorrow, let's go check the outside of the plane to see if it is safe enough to be treated as our new home. I wouldn't want to finally make contact with someone only to come back and find the plane in pieces and parts all the way down the mountain. Every once in a while we've heard creaking but so far it hasn't moved. Hopefully, that's a good thing."

Melina responded, "I'm glad to hear that you're thinking about the safety for the rest of us."

"You're welcome."

The guys went outside and walked around what was left of the plane. They tried rocking it and it didn't move. They looked at each other and signaled thumbs up.

Tuesday, the two of them devised some snow shoes and went walking outside to see if they were durable enough to go long distances. Once they felt comfortable with that, they went inside to gather what gear and supplies they could find. They also had the cell phone that Jean Claude had sent a text message on. Melina was afraid to let them go, but the guys said that the weather was good. Nick said, "If it starts getting bad, we'll return, but we need to try and get out of here."

"Okay. Please take some water bottles from the attendant's cabin. Would you like some pretzels or peanuts?"

Nick said, "That's okay, Melina. I will take the water, but pass on the other stuff."

"Speak for yourself," said Jean Claude and took some peanuts.

That being said, the two of them started heading down the mountain.

Chapter Twelve

Wednesday afternoon Jane drove Marie to the medical clinic in Gothenburg. When the assistant asked how she could help them, Marie introduced herself. "Oh, yes," said the assistant. "Dr. Slischburg said you would be arriving. Please fill out these forms. He is on his way."

The ladies sat down, Jane said, "I have to admit that I was a little pensive when Frank said he was a doctor and wanted to meet us at the address he gave us. He could have been an ax murderer and having us go someplace where he could do bodily harm. I wanted to ask for proof that he was a doctor, but thought better of it. Why would a doctor carry his credentials on a hike?"

"Boy, you really do have a vivid imagination!"

Marie filled out the forms and gave them back to the assistant. She then was escorted back to the x-ray room. A while later, Frank came out to the waiting area and told Jane that it would be about one hour before getting the results. He said, "Would you like to go to the gourmet coffee shop next door and get some coffee? My treat."

"You're a man after my own heart, doctor. My weakness is gourmet coffee, but what about Marie?"

"She's fine. The nurse is taking her vitals and finding more about her medical history."

"If that's occurring, you may want to take me to dinner instead. She has a very long medical history. Just kidding on the dinner, but not on the long history."

Frank just laughed, took Jane's arm and out the door they went.

While at the coffee shop, Frank's cell phone had a text that the x-rays were ready so he and Jane walked back to the medical center. "Do you want to be with Marie when I give her the results?"

"Sure," was the answer.

They went back to the examining room and Frank showed Marie where she had fractured her foot. As he was pointing, "You have a chipped bone in this area; and this area looks like another fracture a while ago."

Marie said, "I did that while we were on a camping trip a few years ago."

"Am I to assume that you weren't planning on staying here very long?"

Jane responded, "You assume correctly as we're leaving the day after tomorrow. Maybe I should ask if Marie would be well enough to leave the day after tomorrow."

"Well, she really should have a plaster cast on that foot for at least six weeks and then have me look at it again at that time. Since that's not in the cards, let's get a walking cast and give you the x-rays. Do you know where you'll be in six weeks?"

Jane asked Marie, "Do you want to wait until we get to your ranch in Albuquerque and see your own doctor?"

"Yes, Jane. If that's okay with you. I don't want to ruin your trip."

"So far, I've been worried that I'm ruining your trip."

Frank chimed in, "Ladies, I've only known you two for a few hours and learned more about you than my own friends."

The ladies together responded, "Sorry, Frank." Jane said, "We've really messed up your day. We hope you weren't going to play golf."

"I'm not the golfing type. More like tennis and downhill skiing."

Jane, said, "I couldn't agree more. My sweetheart keeps trying to teach me, but it's too mental, especially when I get near water. I lose so many balls in the water that I just give up."

Marie said, 'Is there anything else I need to do, Frank?"

"I'll give you a prescription for pain. It will also be a good idea to stay off it as much as possible and keep it elevated when sitting. Please see the assistant out front and she'll give you your x-rays. I wish you both the best of luck; and may you have safe travels."

Jane said, "You've been more than helpful today and we couldn't be more appreciative."

Marie chimed in, "I'll second that. Thank you so much, Frank. Let's get back to our home away from home, Jane. I'm tired and it's been a long day. We may want to check in with Vince to see if he has an update on the plane crash."

Frank asked, "Is that the plane that crashed into the side of a mountain in the Alps?"

Jane responded, "Yes, and my fiancée was on that plane. The air tower lost communication and the rescue teams have been looking for days. I'm so worried that something has happened to him."

"Well, I'm sure he's all right, Jane. Why don't you two come over to my place tonight? It's supposed to be a beautiful evening and I can grill us some steaks out on my back patio. I think you can use some good conversation with others. I'll see if Nick and his girlfriend are available and we'll have a little party."

Jane winced when he said the name of Nick and started to tear up.

Frank said, "Did I say something wrong?"

Marie responded, "That's her fiancée's name."

"I'm so sorry, Jane. Here I was trying to cheer you up and did the exact opposite. Please forgive me."

Jane responded, "That's okay, Frank. You can't change your friend's name. Is Nick the one you were hiking with this morning?"

"Yes, we've been best friends for years. He was especially helpful to me when my wife passed away a few years ago."

"Now I'm the sorry one. We sure are a pair, aren't we."

"Let's start over. Would you two like to come to my place for a cookout this evening, say around 7:00?"

The ladies both responded, sure; and asked if they could bring something.

"You've had enough going on today. Don't worry about bringing anything. See you at 7:00."

The ladies left the medical center and Jane drove the truck back to their campsite. Marie called Vince and woke him up. He said, "So glad you called, Marie. I must have overslept. I've finished my meetings here in Tokyo and am scheduled to leave for Hong Kong, China this afternoon. How are you two travelers doing?"

"WELLLL—Jane and I were hiking this morning and I fell and chipped a bone in my heel. I now have a cast."

"Ohhh my. How are you feeling? Are you in any pain?"

"Fortunately a gentleman and his friend were hiking behind us and one of them is a doctor. He has been a God send and has me all mended, at least for the moment."

"I wish I could be there to take care of you. I guess I'll have to trust Jane. Put your phone on speaker and I'll give an update, although there isn't much news."

Marie put the phone on speaker and Vince said, "The rescue teams were getting exhausted as they had reached one of the summits and found no evidence of the plane. They are going back down the mountain which will take another three days. The command center will send in another six teams and start up again in an adjacent area. This area is more rugged terrain and it's going to take longer to get up the mountain. In the interim, helicopters have been flying all over the mountain and have found no evidence of the plane. They're also looking for any type of signal, such as smoke, flames, or reflection like from a mirror. The FAA marked the flight path and the teams thought they were in the right area but no luck."

Jane asked if the weather was still good. Vince said, "So far it's been sunny but very cold at night. The teams camp out in tents at night and try to keep warm. Fortunately, it's June so the weather stays pretty nice for a few weeks."

Jane responded, "Sure it does. That's why there was a freaky disastrous blizzard that just happened when my sweetheart was flying."

Marie said, "Jane, try to not be so bitter. You keep taking your grief out on Vince."

"I'm a big boy, Marie. I understand why Jane makes snide comments. I can take it if it helps her feel better."

Marie told Vince that they needed to end the call as the ladies were going over to Frank's home for a cookout.

Vince said, "That's some doctor. He mends you up and then feeds you too. Does he also make house calls?"

"Do I hear a sound of jealousy in your voice, sweetheart?"

"Not really; but those westerners must have a different style of medical care."

"We aren't quite to the western states yet."

"Well, you're in western Nebraska and that's close enough."

"Let's try to end this conversation on a positive note. I love you, Vince."

"And I love you, Marie. Miss you loads, goodbye."

Chapter Thirteen

The guys had been walking for about an hour when Jean Claude said, "I saw where you grabbed that cell phone that I used for sending a message. Are you showing any reception on it now?"

"No, but I'll keep checking. I was noticing how you were struggling with breathing in this high altitude. Want to stop for a few minutes?"

"That would probably be a good idea, especially since that leg of yours seems to be getting bigger."

The men walked for another hour and were getting hungry, so they munched on the peanuts and pretzels.

Nick said, "I guess you were smart in taking these munchies."

"I'm assuming you're talking about the peanuts and pretzels."

"Sorry. I should stop using American slang words. I guess you're teaching me some proper grammar. On another note, I'm looking at the cell phone and no bars are showing. I think we should head back up to the plane. Let's see if we can find any type of stuff we can use as cairns on our way back. Hopefully, the rescue teams will come across them."

"What would you suggest? We haven't seen anything but snow. I haven't even seen any animals or tracks but maybe that's a good thing."

"Well, there have been areas where some boulders are showing. Maybe we can carve a message on them with the small screw driver we found in the attendant's cabin."

"Good idea. Let's get started."

As the men headed back up the mountain, they managed to carve messages in three different locations. They spelled out PLANE with an arrow pointing up.

The men managed to get back to the plane just as it was getting dark. Nick's leg was throbbing and Jean Claude felt like his lungs were about to explode.

While the men were gone, Melina managed to find some oxygen for the man who kept drifting in and out of consciousness. She also worked at cleaning up a lot of the debris and made a living-type environment. She didn't have a lot to work with, but managed to put some seats together to make beds for everyone.

When the guys came back, Melina said, "You two look terrible. Please sit over here and I'll take a look at what damages you have caused yourselves."

The men responded, "Thanks for the reassurance."

Melina saw where Jean Claude's back was bleeding. She also noticed that Nick's leg was really swollen. She pressed on it and he flinched. She said, "I'm afraid this is getting worse, Nick. I didn't want to tell you before, but I'm afraid there's a blood clot and you may also have internal bleeding. I do have some blood thinners you can take but you need to be regimented and take them every day to try and dissolve the blood clot. I can't do anything about the internal bleeding. I would say to stay off of it, but know that's not going to happen."

Melina went back to the attendant's station and boiled some water. She tended to Jean Claude's back and redressed the wound.

Nick said to Melina, "I like what you've done to the place. You're quite an interior designer."

"Very funny, Nick," was her response. "Did you make any contact with anyone by going down the mountain?"

"Regrettably, no. However, we did manage to carve some messages into boulders on our way back. The writing is pretty big, so hopefully aircraft will see it and get a message back to the command center. At least I'm assuming that there is a command center. I don't know about Jean Claude, but I'm very hungry. Is there any food left or did you and John Doe have a party while we were gone?"

Melina said, "You must have found your humor while you were out on that mountain. I'll be glad to fix you something as long as you stay in that chair and keep your leg propped up."

"Yes, mam."

"Jean Claude, while I'm playing chef, would you mind putting John Doe on that couch over there? I think he'll be more comfortable than lying on the floor."

"No problem."

While they were all eating, Melina said, "I know that I nixed the idea of building a fire; but should we at least try?"

Jean Claude responded, "No. 1, I don't think we have much to build a fire; No. 2, it would just melt the snow; No. 3, It wouldn't last long enough for anyone to see it."

Nick said, "You always put a damper on our Wheaties."

"And what does that mean. Is that another one of your idioms?"

"Yes, it is. Sorry. I think we've accomplished enough for one day. Let's try and get some rest in these newly decorated living quarters. We can regroup tomorrow and see what new ideas we can conjure up."

Chapter Fourteen

The ladies made their way over to Frank's home that evening. Frank greeted them at the door. Jane said, "What a lovely home."

"My wife and I looked for many months and when we walked to the front door of this house, she said this was going to be the one. I had to agree with her. We've had many happy memories in this home."

Marie asked, "Do you have any children?"

"No. The rabbit refused to die, but we enjoyed our dogs. You'll meet the two of them when we go out back to the patio."

As they walked to the back of the house, the two dogs came running. "I guess they didn't want to wait until we made it to the patio." The dogs were jumping up on Jane and almost knocked Marie over.

"I'm so sorry, Marie. Please sit over here and I'll take the dogs outside before I need to mend you again."

Marie said, "That's not necessary. I'm clumsy to begin with; and then to have this walking cast on my foot doesn't help my balance."

Nick and his girlfriend were already out on the patio. They came inside to see what the commotion was all about.

Nick commented, "Are your dogs causing trouble again, Frank?"

"Of course. They love people, especially women. I can't say that I blame them. Jane and Marie, this is Nick's girlfriend, Elana." The ladies exchanged greetings and Frank said, "Nick, let's go out to the patio and I'll take the dogs with us so they don't cause any more trouble. Ladies, would you mind going to the kitchen and pouring the wine while I start the grill? The wine and glasses are already on the counter. I also made a fruit and cheese platter. You can find that in the refrigerator."

Jane said, "Well, aren't you the efficient one."

"I don't know about being efficient. My wife always used to handle preparations for guests. My job was always the grill."

After dinner, they all sat around the fire pit and shared hiking stories. Jane said, "It's getting late and we need to get Marie back to the campground. This has been very pleasant, Frank. I've probably said it before, but you've done more than enough. First, we were fortunate to have you come along and take care of Marie's foot. Then you treated us to a delicious steak dinner when it should have been us that did the treating. We will never be able to thank you enough."

"I second that," said Marie.

"No thanks are necessary," responded Frank. I thoroughly enjoyed your company, Jane; and you too, Marie. I only wish you two were here longer so I can further tend to Marie's foot."

Jane said, "Let me see what I can do with our itinerary. I had us doing a lot of sightseeing in Moab and Provo, Utah. With Marie incapacitated, there's probably no sense spending two weeks in those areas. After Marie and I discuss our change in plans, I'll call you."

As Frank was walking with the ladies to the front door, he said, "I'll look forward to it." He took Marie's hand, kissed it and let go. Then he looked at Jane. For a moment, it looked like he wanted to pull her close to him and kiss her on the lips. He thought better of it and just took her hand in his, held it, looked into her eyes, then let go. "Drive safely ladies." He watched them as they walked back to the truck.

On the way back to the campground, Marie said, "I don't think it would be a good idea for us to stay here six more weeks. With the way Frank looks at you, it could evolve into something very dangerous. Besides, what on earth can we do here in Gothenburg, Nebraska that long? Sounds boring and I'm going to be bored as it is with sitting all of the time."

"Frank is just being gracious, Marie. You have nothing to worry about; but I do agree with you. Staying in this town would get old very quick. I'll call him tomorrow and tell him that we will stick to our present itinerary."

Thursday morning, Jane went outside and called Frank to let him know they were going to leave on Friday. "I'm sorry to hear that, Jane. I'm worried about Marie's foot healing properly. It's always good to stay with one doctor during an injury, but I understand why you wouldn't want to be here for six weeks. I have trouble keeping myself entertained and educated in this small community of only 7,000 people. I've often thought of moving to a larger city, but these people depend on me. A hospital in Sacramento, California keeps sending me offers, but I just toss them."

"You are too talented for this town. You really should reconsider their offer. It's probably double what you're making now."

"Actually, it's triple. Then, there's my home. I don't know if I can give it up. I think of my wife whenever I walk into a room."

"Then that's another reason for taking the offer."

"You're so easy to talk to, Jane. Would you consider meeting me at the gourmet coffee shop this afternoon to just talk?"

"I don't think that's a good idea. You've become a great friend in such a short time; and I'm afraid you might want more if we continue. I have a wonderful fiancée and am worried sick about him."

"I'm so sorry. I haven't even asked if you've heard any good news."

"Not really. There are six rescue teams of six and no one has found any evidence of the plane."

"My thoughts and prayers will be with you and your sweetheart, Jane. Have a safe trip. Goodbye."

"Goodbye, Frank. Marie and I will always remember you." With that, Jane hung up the cell phone.

She went back inside and Marie was making coffee. "Was that Frank that you were talking to so long?"

"Yes, but it wasn't really that long. I told him that we aren't changing our itinerary and that we're leaving tomorrow."

"That's good, Jane. I know Nick is your life and I have a feeling Frank would end up being the one that's hurt."

"No one's getting hurt. Let's change the subject. What would you like to do today? We can go to the Visitor's Center in North Platte. I'm sure they would have wheelchairs there."

"WOW—that's way up there on my bucket list. I guess there's nothing else to do, unless we left for Cheyenne, Wyoming today. I believe you said its only 170 miles away."

"I think you should rest one more day."

"Yes, Mother."

Chapter Fifteen

By the following Friday, Nick, Jean Claude and Melina were getting concerned that no one would find them. The food was almost gone and still they weren't able to find any working communication. The gentleman with amnesia had finally calmed down, due in part to Melina's happy pills. Jean Claude and Melina were the best of the group as Nick's leg was getting worse. He was having trouble walking on it but wouldn't give up.

That afternoon, they heard voices. It was one of the rescue teams. The lead man, George, called from the outside. "Is anyone in there?"

In unison, they shouted, "YES, YES, YES. Please come in."

As George and the team entered, he commented, "My, you really know how to survive in the worst of conditions. You'll have to give us some lessons. How many of you survived?"

Nick said, "What you see is what you get. After the plane crashed, there were six of us and now we're down to four. Melina is a registered nurse and had just come back from a medical conference, so she has lots of medical supplies and equipment. Otherwise, there would probably be only one or two of us left. The pilot and crew did not survive the crash. With it hitting the mountain, only those of us at the rear of the plane survived."

George said, "I noticed the pile of bodies outside. We're so sorry that you had to deal with that. There's a helicopter coming for you. We need to do it quickly as there's another bad storm coming. It's unusual for such bad storms at this time of year. It will take you to Paris as they have some of the best medical facilities in Western Europe. I can see that your leg needs to be addressed rather quickly. By the way, did anyone fine the black box?"

Melina said, "No. I'm the registered nurse that's been tending to everyone. That man lying over there has a bad gash on his head. He just mumbles and drifts in and out of consciousness. We don't know his name or anything else, for that matter."

Just then, the helicopter made a tenuous landing in the snow. Lots of it was flying everywhere. Nick tried getting up but was struggling so George helped him to the chopper. Needless to say, Nick wasn't pleased that he wasn't able to help himself and was really worried about his leg. George went after John Doe who woke up and started screaming again. George managed to calm him down and then carried him to the helicopter. Jean Claude and Melina followed; and off they flew to Paris. While in the air, Nick whispered to George, "*I have a fiancée in the states, but don't want her to know that I've been hurt. Can you tell the doctors that I was already on the chopper when you got the others and report that only three survived?*"

George responded, "*And how do you suggest that I keep you out of the media?*"

"You can say that I was already on the chopper when you picked up the others so you don't need to mention my name or count me as one of the survivors. Say only three made it."

"I'll see what I can do. By the way, what is your name again?"

"I'm Nicholas Cambini."

Nick then talked to Jean Claude and Melina. "I'm pretty sure that the doctors are going to have to cut off my leg. I don't want to be a burden to my sweetheart so PLEASE don't say that I was on the plane. I want her to think that I didn't survive."

Jean Claude said, "Do you think that's fair to your sweetheart?"

"Being fair has nothing to do with it. I have lots of money and will take care of her financially. She'll be happier without the burden of an invalid."

"Such a martyr, you are Mr. Nick."

"I agree," was the response of Melina.

"I don't care what any of you think. This is the way it's going down. Not another word."

Jean Claude responded, "There he goes again with that idiom."

Once they reached the hospital in Paris, Nick called his assistant and said. "I need you to create dummy identification with the name of Nicholas Cambini and overnight it to me at this hospital. UNDER NO CIRCUMSTANCES ARE YOU TO TELL ANYONE THAT I'M ALIVE. If anyone finds out, including Jane, you will be fired. Do you understand?"

"Yes sir." The assistant did as he was told. To anyone who asked for proof of identification, Nick said it was lost when the plane crashed and he was getting duplicates.

Chapter Sixteen

That Friday morning, the ladies got up around 8:00AM. Jane asked Marie how her foot was doing. "It's fine, Jane. Quit worrying about me. You know that I'm an old pro at these things."

"Well, I know that you're old, but being a pro at something is another story."

"Very funny. Let's get some breakfast and then head off to Cheyenne. In fact, let's just go to your Gourmet hangout and have a light breakfast with your high-test coffee. You look like you can use some energy."

Once they arrived at the Gourmet Shop, there was Frank having coffee with Nick. He said, "It's nice to see you ladies this morning. Nick and I just finished our walk. Would you like to join us?"

"Of course," was Jane's answer. She and Marie sat opposite the men. Frank said, "I thought you were leaving this morning."

Jane responded, "We are but only have to travel 170 miles so thought we would just have breakfast here."

"I'm so glad. How's that foot doing, Marie? You can really maneuver around with that walking cast. I guess you don't listen to a doctor's advice when he/she tells you something. I believe I said to stay off it as much as possible. Do you want me to take a look at it?"

"No, you don't need to look at it; and I have been sitting a lot. In fact, I'll be sitting most of today."

"Well, someone is a little testy. I guess we need to change the subject. Have either of you ever been to Cheyenne?"

Jane said she had been there years ago, but Marie had never experienced it. Frank told them that there is a rodeo in July that is known as the world's largest outdoor rodeo. "It's a shame that you're going to miss it. They say, it's the daddy of them all. You could stay here an extra three weeks and then go to Cheyenne."

Jane said, "We can't stay here and we only planned on staying in Cheyenne the weekend. We need to be back at Marie's ranch in Albuquerque by mid August. Her husband is on a business trip for a few weeks and will be anxious to have her back home. They still haven't found my fiancée but I know that he also will be waiting for me."

"Of course he will. Well, ladies, it was a pleasure to see you again, but I need to get to the medical clinic." Nick said that he also needed to get back to work.

With that, the men left. The ladies finished with their breakfast and headed back to the campground. They were on the road by 10:00 and made it to Cheyenne with no trouble. Jane took over Marie's duties of setting up the camp while Marie went inside and tended to things she could do while sitting down. She was frustrated and said, "There isn't much of anything one can do sitting down. This is stupid. I'm going to take off this walking cast and do the inside arrival chores."

"Don't you dare take that cast off. You're a pro at getting around on that thing. Leave it on and do the best you can. Yell, if you need help. I'm going to set up the chairs outside. You fix us some drinks and your famous pu-pu platter."

"Why do the Hawaiians call it that anyhow? It doesn't sound very appealing."

"I'll ask my Hawaiian son-in-law the next time that I see him."

Once the ladies were outside in their chairs, Jane was browsing through some literature she had picked up at the campground office. "I'm looking at the local happening events. There's the Frontier Days Old West Museum and we can see Old Number 4004. It's supposed to be the world's largest railroad steam engine. Maybe I could push you in a wheelchair while walking through some of the Medicine Bow National Forest. It's supposed to have beautiful rock formations."

"Man, you really know how to show a lady a fun time; but I'm going to have to pass on all of that stuff. Is that all there is?"

"I'm going to suggest something that doesn't have any walking and I won't like to do it but, such a friend I am. How about I find us some horses to ride? I'm sure Wyoming has horses."

"Ohhh my, Jane. Would you really do that for me?"

"What are friends for." Jane went over to the campground office to inquire about horseback riding. The owners gave her a brochure and said it wasn't far from the campground.

The next day the ladies ventured off to go horseback riding. They had to walk far to find the stables and

Marie's foot was throbbing. "Before we ride, Jane, I think we'd better find a bench someplace and let me put my foot up for a while."

"I'm sorry, Marie. I promised you no walking and here we are tending to your foot. So much for no walking."

They found a bench in the beautiful riding stable. Jane said, "You had better appreciate this one. As you know, my former husband and I owned four horses. The only time he got me to ride was after I had downed some Scotch. I don't enjoy or appreciate the beauty of horses."

Just then, a cowboy walked up to the ladies and said, "I don't have any Scotch in the stables; but no need to worry, as our horses are pretty tame. I'm sure you'll enjoy the ride."

Marie said, "As you can see, I'm in a walking cast. Would it be too much trouble for you to help me get on the horse? I used to ride years ago, but my friend here is not quite sure she wants to get on a horse."

"That's why we're here." Then the cowboy helped the ladies get up on the horses. "These Morgans are passive, ladies, so you'll be fine on the trail. It's marked pretty well; but here's a trail map in case you get lost. Do you have cell phones?"

"Yes, we do."

"That's good. Program the stable telephone number just as a precaution. One can never be too careful."

As the ladies were going down the marked trail, Jane said, "That cowboy back at the stables seemed to be paranoid about our safety. It makes me wonder what type of trail we're heading toward."

"There you go again, being worried about something that probably could never happen."

"Okay. I'll reboot, as they say. This area is really beautiful and I suppose we wouldn't have seen it via a motor vehicle. I'm just going to resort to the fact that horseback riding can be enjoyable."

"There are so many things to see while riding a horse. You always appreciate nature, Jane, and this is one perfect way to see it."

"Actually, I prefer the hiking on foot route, but I'll grin and bear this mode of transportation, just for you."

As Jane was talking, she got knocked off her horse by a tree limb. It hit her in the head and knocked her out.

Marie got off her horse and hobbled over to Jane. "Jane, Jane, can you hear me?" There was no response. She tried slapping Jane on the face but nothing happened. The noise spooked the horses and they ran away. *Now what do I do,* thought Marie. She sat there for a few minutes and then slapped Jane on the face again. She finally woke up.

"Why did you have to slap me on the face? It hurts."

"You were knocked out and I kept trying to revive you. There's a big bump on your head. Do you remember hitting that tree over there?"

"I only remember talking to you and then you were slapping me. I'll bet that was fun."

"As a matter of fact, it was."

Jane asked, "Where are the horses?"

"Something spooked them and they ran off."

"That's just dandy." Jane tried to stand up but collapsed on the ground. "I told you that I don't like to ride horses. This wouldn't happen if we were shopping at some beautiful boutiques."

"Quit grumbling. Fortunately the cowboy gave us a number if something happened. I wondered why he was so cautious about our cell phones working. It's like he had a premonition." Marie made the telephone call and the ladies waited under the tree.

It seemed like hours before anyone came. They saw two horses with riders coming over the ridge. One was the cowboy that had helped them at the riding stables and the other one was a doctor. Jane said, "This is too much."

The men got off their horses and the cowboy said, "We've never had anyone be hit by a tree on this range. You're pretty talented, mam."

"I'm not a mam. My name is Jane; and riding horses is not my cup of tea."

"I can see that. Apparently, I should have given you more guidance before tackling these trails."

"I was doing just fine. I just happened to get distracted and wasn't paying attention. I'm fine and I don't need any doctor to look at me."

"You're here at our riding stables and we don't take kindly to anyone getting hurt. Can you stand up?"

"Of course I can." Jane started to get up and fell down again. That's when the doctor took a look at her. He said, "I think it's a concussion, but we may need to perform a CT scan. Let's get her back to the medical facility and I'll examine her further."

Once they were back at the medical facility, the CT scan was performed. The doctor said, "You have a slight concussion but I found nothing else wrong. However, you cannot drive."

"Marie, do you think you can drive us back to our campground?"

"Sure. It's not far and I remember how easy it was to find this place. The campground owners made a fine recommendation."

The next morning, Jane was directed back to the medical facility to make sure she was able to drive. The doctor checked her over and said, "You healed fast, mam. Everything looks good. Again, we're very sorry for your mishap. Hopefully, you won't blame the horse."

"I'm fine and I won't blame the horse. However, I don't plan on ever riding again, thank you very much. Is the concussion gone; and am I able to drive?"

"Yes, on both counts. Have safe journeys."

The ladies bid a fond farewell to the doctor and Jane drove them drove back to their campground.

That evening they were sitting outside and watching the beautiful sunset. "There's really nothing more beautiful than a west's sunset. Don't you agree, Marie?"

"You are absolutely correct."

"Well, you should feel better now. I've finally visited a medical facility."

"While that's true, you have a very long way to go to catch up with me."

"I hope you don't mind, but that's one thing I don't care to do."

"I entirely understand. Let's put out the fire and call it a day. We aren't young chicks anymore and don't bounce back from healing like we did in years ago."

"Agreed."

The following Monday morning, the ladies were on the road by 10:00AM headed for Estes Park, Colorado.

Chapter Seventeen

At the hospital in Paris, a team of specialists looked at Nick's leg. The lead doctor explained to Nick that the crash damaged his leg so badly that it had to be removed. "Gangrene is starting to set in. If we don't remove it, you may lose your life instead of your leg. "

"I don't really care what you do. I've lost my sweetheart either way and she was my life."

"Sign these papers and we will start the operation immediately."

Nick signed the papers as Nicholas Cambini and the doctor left the room.

Melina passed the doctor as she was heading to Nick's room. He said, "Your friend is very depressed. We have a serious operation to perform and I'm concerned that he won't make it. That seems to be his wish anyhow."

"I'll talk to him, doctor. I've been told that your team is great at what they do so we can only hope for the best." With that, Melina entered Nick's room and he wouldn't even look at her.

"Hello, Nick. We are so grateful to have been found in that very remote area. You and Jean Claude were ingenious to carve messages in the boulders. I'm so thankful that you saved us. By the way, Jean Claude is in the next room. I guess his back is pretty bad. They are concerned that he damaged some organs."

"And what do you want me to do about it?"

"Nothing. I just thought you'd like to know how all of us are doing."

"Well, you have two legs and moving around quite nicely. Lucky you."

Melina thought, *I just want to shake him and say quit feeling sorry for yourself, but that would only agitate him more. I guess I'll just bite my tongue.*

"Things will get better, Nick, and you'll be back with your sweetheart in no time."

"I'm never going back to the states. If I do survive this operation, which I hope I don't, then I'm going back to my home in Italy. Now get out of here and leave me alone. I don't want to see any of you ever again."

Melina left the room and went to visit Jean Claude who was next door. "Jean Claude, I'm so worried about Nick. He is so depressed and doesn't want to live. Since they have to amputate his leg, he feels that he'll be of no use to his fiancée. Can you talk to him?"

"The doctors don't want me to move for a few days. You did a great job on my back with the supplies and knowledge that you had. However, I guess the crash impacted some of the organs and they want to wait a few days to see how they are healing. Just let Nick rest. We've all been in shock these past few days and all need time to get over what we've been through."

"I guess you're right. By the way, when I told Nick that you were in the next room and the doctors were concerned about your organs, he responded saying 'and what do you want me to do about it?' I thought he would want to know all of our conditions but is just feeling sorry for himself. I don't know how to help him."

"Like I said, give him time. How is our other male companion doing? Were they able to find out who he is?"

"I guess he's still not talking. They took a brain scan and there is some pressure on the right side of his brain. They are trying to relieve it."

"So, I guess you are okay. When will you be released?"

"They said I can go tomorrow. I don't know if I told you but I'm originally from Switzerland. I came here years ago to finish my medical schooling and never left. I have an apartment here in town. Surprisingly, I was trained at this hospital, but now work just outside of Paris. I assume, from your name, that you live around here."

"Yes, I do. I also have an apartment in the city. I went to visit some friends in Switzerland and was on my way back when the tragedy occurred."

"That's a good way to put it. I'll come to visit you and Nick. Maybe when you're released, I can visit you at your home and help your convalescence."

I'd like that; and will look forward to it. I'm assuming, from your conversation, that you don't have a husband or significant other."

"Not at the present time. I had a relationship for a few years, but it didn't work out."

The nurse entered the room to draw blood and take stats so Melina told Jean Claude that she would see him tomorrow. She then went to visit John Doe. The doctors were looking him over so Melina said she would come back later.

Chapter Eighteen

While on the road, the ladies heard on the radio that the rescue team had found the plane and there were only three survivors. They gave no names so Jane asked Marie to call Vince. "It's 2:00AM in Tokyo, Jane."

"I don't care. I'm surprised that Vince hasn't called us with this great news."

"Maybe he doesn't know it yet."

"I would think with his connections, that he would know it before the media found out."

"You're getting testy again. Okay, I'm calling him now."

Marie dialed the number and Vince answered in a sleepy tone. "I'm sorry to call you so late, Vince, but we just heard that they found three survivors but don't have any names. Do you have any information?"

"I'm afraid that I do, Marie, and it isn't good. I wanted to wait until you were parked at a campsite. Nick's name is not among the living." Marie tried hard not to show any emotion so said, "You go back to sleep, sweetheart. We'll be in Estes Park, Colorado in about four hours. Will you have information by then?"

He pretended to answer yes and Marie hung up. "What did Vince tell you, Marie?"

"I'm afraid he was too sleepy to be coherent so he will call us this afternoon."

As soon as they found their campground and were settled, Jane asked Marie to call Vince again. "Vince is working and may be in a meeting, Jane. He said he would call us so be patient."

"How can I be patient when I don't know if Nick is alive or dead?"

Just then Marie's cell phone rang and she answered it. She told Vince that it was on speaker so Jane could also hear what he had to say. "From what I gathered, one of the survivors had carved a message in a boulder and a plane flying over the area reported it back to a command center set up in Bern. A helicopter managed to land in a remote area right by the remnants of the plane. I guess the plane hit front end into the mountain. The pilot, crew and most of the passengers died on impact. The crew leader from the rescue team was told that six people survived the crash but only three people boarded the helicopter. He didn't mention what happened to the other three."

Jane said, "Come on, Vince, and tell me one of them was Nick that boarded the chopper."

"I'm afraid not, Jane."

There was a long pause. Marie looked at Jane. She was just sitting there. Vince asked what was going on.

Jane responded, "I'm sure Nick is alive. I can feel it in my bones. Maybe he had gone down the mountain looking for help. I'm not giving up."

Vince chimed in, "You're probably absolutely right, Jane. Nick's the type of guy that won't just sit around and wait for someone to come. I'll keep abreast with my informants. I should have known that you wouldn't give up. I'm getting ready to pack and head for China. Do you know when you two will be at the ranch in Albuquerque?"

Marie responded, "We are still on schedule so, if nothing goes awry, we should be there towards the middle of August."

"Will you be back for your birthday? I have something special planned."

"Of course you do. I would expect nothing less. We'll try. I'm sure that I'll be talking to you many times before then so you will know the exact date as it gets closer to that time." That being said, they ended the conversation.

As the ladies were sitting around the evening fire, Jane's cell phone rang and it was Frank. "Jane, I heard on the news that they found three survivors. I'm afraid to ask---" Jane interrupted him and said, "Nick's name was not one of the three but I'm sure that he's still alive. I'm convinced that he went down the mountain to find help. I'll be hearing from him shortly."

"Of course you will. On another note, I want you to know that I took your advice. I've taken that job in Sacramento and leave next month. I've put my home on the market."

"WOW, Frank, that's great news. I know both of those things were huge decisions for you. Congratulations!"

"Well, we'll see how things shake out. I wouldn't have been able to do it without your support. Didn't you say that you ladies have a trip scheduled to arrive in Sacramento around that time?"

"Yes, we do. Text me the name and telephone number of the hospital and we'll look you up when we get there."

"This is so exciting, Jane. I can't tell you how long it's been since I was excited about anything. I need to move on with my life and hope I've made the right decision."

"I'm sure it is, Frank. I need to stoke the fire, so have a great evening, Goodbye."

"Goodbye, Jane."

After Jane hung up, Marie asked, "Was that Frank?"

"Yes, it was." She proceeded to explain the news to Marie, who thought, *"I suppose this is the best thing for Jane right now. My only concern is if Nick is alive, what a spider web will be woven."*

"Now you're on my turf, Marie. I know it's difficult for you to walk long distances but there's still lots we can do. We can ride go-carts or shop downtown as they have wheelchairs. We can do that tomorrow. Then Thursday I'll take you for a ride along Trail Ridge Road Highway. It's one of the most scenic routes in the country. You'll get to see a panoramic view of the great Rockies and Continental Divide. Friday we head for Central City. My close friends, Jim and George, would take me there and meet lots of the local folk. We had some fun times in that town over the years. I can't wait for you to meet them. Once we arrive, I'll call and have them meet us in town. You can experience what knowledge they have on the town and its surroundings. We'll probably spend the night in one of the old hotels with furniture dating back to the 1800s."

"I hope the mattresses aren't that old."

"HAH-HAH!"

Tuesday the ladies stayed around the campground and did some cleaning. The next task was to wash clothes. There was a nice laundry facility at the campground, so they read their books while waiting for the clothes to wash and dry. Once that chore was finished, they drove into town for a nice steak dinner.

Wednesday was go-cart day. The two of them were adversaries, once they were in the carts. They kept bumping into each other on purpose. Jane finally told Marie to chill or she would be getting a whip lash. "You're just worried that I'm going to beat you," was her reply.

Once they finished that sport, they drove through the town and found a handicapped spot to park. Jane told Marie to wait in the car while she looked for a wheelchair. She walked down the street and found the Chamber of Commerce. She asked where she could locate a wheelchair to rent. "My friend has a cast on her foot and I'd like to show her the sites." The clerk said that they had one available for free. "You just need to return it by 6:00 as that's when we close." Jane thanked the lady and wheeled the chair back to the car. Marie was grateful that she didn't have to walk as her foot was aching.

As Jane was pushing the wheelchair down the sidewalk, Marie said, "This is such a quaint town and the area is gorgeous. How could you leave this beautiful state and move back to Ohio?"

"It was more of a financial decision as opposed to an emotional one. I've explained it to you over the years, so let's not belabor the point and just enjoy our shopping."

As they entered one of the boutiques, Jane bumped into an old friend. "Lisa, how wonderful to see you!"

"WOW, I don't believe my eyes. I haven't seen you in years, Jane. What are you doing here?"

"This is my friend, Marie. We are traveling together across the United States in a recreational vehicle and having a blast. Do you have time to join us for a late lunch? I'd love to find out how you and your family are doing. I really miss your kids and that awful husband of yours."

"My awful husband is fine and the kids still talk about their adopted Aunt Jane. I need to pick up some things. Can you meet me over at the Tomato Skin Restaurant, say at 3:00? It's just down one block and around the corner."

Jane looked at Marie and asked, "Is that okay with you, Marie?" Marie shook her head, yes; and Lisa went her way.

Marie commented, "She seems like a nice lady."

"She and her husband helped me when I was near bankruptcy and nearly lost my home near here. It was at a very low point in my life, but I will be forever grateful to them."

"How did the awful husband help if he was so bad."

"I was being facetious. He and Lisa took me into their home while I rented my fully furnished one to a nice young couple. When I returned to Ohio and landed that job at the commercial firm, I sold my home that was near here. It seems every time I leave Ohio, my life is crappy; and every time I go back, it's great. I guess the dear Lord wants me in Ohio for some reason."

"Well, I'm glad he does or I would never have met you. Fate always plays a hand in our lives. Let's finish shopping and go chat with that nice friend of yours."

Thursday, Jane called Jim and asked if he and George could meet them at their favorite saloon in Central City. "Of course we can. We're so excited to see you again and catch up on old times."

The ladies were already at the saloon when the guys showed up. Jane introduced them to Marie. Jim said, "I see that you have a bum foot, Marie. Did Jane drop a boulder on it?"

"That would be a good story, but actually I tripped while we were hiking a few days ago. Jane insists that I motor around in a wheelchair. She says the more I stay off of it, the quicker it will heal."

"It's not me that says it, but that nice doctor we met in Gothenburg, Nebraska."

George commented, "That sounds like a swinging town. I'll bet you had a blast with nothing to do there."

"Actually, it wasn't too bad. They really had nice hiking trails and you guys know how I love to hike. I was always dragging you two up to our favorite spot near Breckenridge over the years."

George looked at Marie and said, "Jane never let us rest on weekends. She was always having us do something. I have to admit that I really miss those weekends. Jim never wants to do anything."

The four of them had a nice dinner and then the guys took them to some quaint stores and saloons.

Marie said, "Jane, I think we had better head back to camp. I regret that I'm getting tired and we need to leave in the morning."

The guys said that it was still early and really wanted them to spend the night in that old hotel Jane had talked about. Jim said, "We haven't seen you in years, Jane. Can't you please stay one more day?"

"We really should be moving on, guys. You see, Marie has a wonderful husband and ranch in Albuquerque and we need to be there by mid August, but I have an idea. Tomorrow, we are heading for Glenwood Springs. You can come to the campground there and spend the weekend with us. We have a large RV and have plenty of room. It'll be fun."

The guys looked at each other and shook their heads, yes. Jane told them that she would text the address to them.

Chapter Nineteen

The ladies made their way to Glenwood Springs the next morning. As they reached Glenwood Canyon, Marie couldn't get over the scenery and how the interstate was constructed. "Jane, I don't think I've ever seen an interstate highway having two lanes over the other two, with each going in opposite directions."

"There is a long story about this part of the interstate. For years, it was just a regular two lane road with 45MPH speed limit in most areas. There was the canyon wall, the road and the Colorado River. On the other side of the river there were the railroad tracks and the other canyon wall. Many travelers wanted to go 70MPH. The transportation department came up with this ingenious way to solve the problem, but the locals had a fit. They said that 70MPH would ultimately destroy the canyon walls due to pollution and fought it for many years. You can see that they ended up losing the battle. It's too beautiful to drive at 70MPH but that's progress."

"I agree with you. It surely is beautiful."

The ladies made it to their next campground in a timely manner. They pulled into the campground and were pleasantly surprised to see the beautiful facility. "This is one of our better places where we've stayed. Don't you agree, Jane?"

"Yes. We're near Aspen, so apparently there are rich campers who like a nice facility."

The camp store was designed with an A-frame. As they entered, they felt like they were in an expensive hunting lodge.

Jane said, "This campground wasn't in my directory so I went online. Believe it or not, the sites are very reasonable. I guess the owners make their money from all of the amenities."

Once they checked in, they drove to their site. Along the way, they saw a swimming pool with swim-through caves, fountains, and swim-up bar. There was also a mini-golf course, shuffleboard and tennis courts. "The guys will go nuts over these facilities," said Jane. "I love playing tennis with Jim because I usually beat him; and he always wanted to play racquetball, as he would usually beat me at that sport. There's so much to see and do here, Marie. We could stay for weeks and never do it all. Downtown has a large outdoor pool that's hot mineral water. I felt greasy after I went swimming in it when I visited years ago. Then, there's Snowmass Ski Area. Further up the road is trendy Aspen. However, we have to stick to the itinerary and stay only three days. There's so much to see and do all the way to Albuquerque."

They arrived at their site and couldn't believe their eyes. "My goodness, Marie. We have a large concrete pad; and look at that nice patio set. We won't even need our folding lounge chairs. The campground already provided them to us. The fire pit is just an added bonus; and look at the stacked wood in that holding ring. I think I've died and gone to heaven."

"I'm so glad to hear the excitement in your voice, Jane. That hasn't happened much since the horrible news."

The ladies performed their arrival duties and then sat down on the patio furniture. "Just look at the beauty all around us. How long did you say that we were staying here, Jane?"

"Just our typical scheduling. We need to leave Thursday for Moab, Utah. That's a breathtaking area and we can't miss Arches National Monument. I've been there. It's a hike and I hope your foot will be up to it."

"It's getting better every day. Quit worrying about me. Speaking of worrying, I'm so proud of how you're handling not hearing from Nick. That has to be a constant worry."

"I know that he's fine. He's probably still going down that mountain for help and doesn't know that the rest have been found. He's a survivor and has spectacular armed services survival skills. He's fine. I know it."

The ladies went inside to prepare appetizers for the men. Jane said, "I'll prepare my crab dip and also Bacon-Water-Chestnut Wraps. Those are two of their favorites. You can work on the cheese platter. I'm sure Jim will be willing to grill the steaks we bought the other day. That built-in barbeque grill at the end of our site is enormous. I'm so glad that I don't have to crawl under the RV to hook up our little grill."

There was a knock at the door and it was the guys. The ladies invited them in and then showed them the interior. The men were impressed with the cathedral ceiling, the breakfast bar, and fireplace in the living room area. "You even have surround sound and a large flat-screen television," said Jim.

"All the comforts of home," was Jane's reply.

The guys mixed some drinks while the ladies took the food outside. When the guys went outside, George said, "My, you ladies really know how to live. This RV is nicer than our apartment. I've never traveled in an RV and am so impressed with this campground."

Jane replied, "Well, this is one of the best that we've ever stayed at and we've been doing this for three years." She then said, "Jim, are you up to a tennis match tomorrow morning?"

"Sure," was his answer. "Only, if we can find a racquetball Club. I wouldn't be surprised to find one in Snowmass or Aspen."

Jane just laughed at his response and said, "You just want to win at something, since you know that it won't be at tennis."

"HAH," was Jim's response.

They all sat around the fire pit all evening and talked of old times. Marie was jealous that she couldn't have been a part of their fun all those many years ago. It started getting cooler so everyone helped carry the leftovers inside. They enjoyed a nightcap and then helped make up beds for the guys.

Tuesday morning Jane and Jim played a few sets on the tennis court while Marie and George played mini golf. That afternoon they all drove to Aspen to tour the town. Marie had never been and was in awe of the surroundings and many boutiques. "I could get used to this type of living real fast," was her answer.

Wednesday, they all went to the Glenwood Springs outdoor pool. It was a beautiful morning. While chatting with each other, Marie commented, "You're right, Jane, about the greasy feeling. Actually, I think it's more of an oily feeling which is good for the skin."

That afternoon, the men said that they needed to get back to Denver. Jim hugged Marie and then looked lovingly at Jane. "I've missed you so much, Jane, but understand why you had to leave our beautiful state. We sure had some fun times, didn't we?"

"Yes, we did, Jim." She gave him a great big hug and kissed him on the cheek. She did the same to George. "You two have a safe trip back to Denver. We'll keep in touch and I promise not to wait so many years until I see you two again."

As the men drove away, Marie said, "You were so blessed to have experienced the friendship of those two. They have so much knowledge of Colorado history. What fascinating individuals. Thank you for letting me be a part of enjoying their company."

"What did you think I would do? Tell you to go find a motel while I visited with the guys?"

"Of course not, but I did feel a little uncomfortable at first. That quickly faded as they were so friendly and made me feel like a part of the group."

"Well, I feel the same way when we travel to an area where you introduce me to your long lost friends and family. That's what's so much fun with this traveling. We each get to see family and friends that we haven't seen in years. Let's make a drink, go sit outside and recap the past few days. I haven't said it in a long time, but I'm so glad that you like to do this travel thing, Marie."

"That's a big ditto to you, good friend."

Chapter Twenty

Nick operation was a success but with any amputation, there is a concern over the healing process. As a result, much against Nick's wishes, the specialists kept him in the hospital an additional three weeks. He hated the world and everyone in it so was not a cooperative patient. The nurses were all grateful when they heard that he was being discharged. The doctors encouraged him to go through a rehabilitation program but Nick refused. His older sister, Agostina, had flown from Italy to visit with him. She tried to convince him to go with her to her home in Italy for a few weeks. "Just until you can survive on your own again."

"I'm doing just fine, Tina," said Nick. (He called her that from the time when he was a child as he had trouble saying her full name.) I've been walking through the hospital with these stupid crutches and I've checked into having a prosthesis fitted to my leg. If there's anything good that has happened with this tragedy, it's that they only needed to amputate to just below the knee. The physical therapist in the rehab department said the prosthesis should be an easy fit. Lucky me.

I'm going to my chalet and hire a physical therapist. In fact, I'm leaning toward hiring Franceau. He's the one that's been working with me in the Rehab Department. Gabrilla has been taking care of my chalet whenever I'm in the states. I'm sure she'll be willing to continue her duties. I don't need anyone else; and if you dare tell Jane that I'm alive, I'll disown you."

"You're not being fair to Jane. She is such a blessing to you and would be of immense help in your convalescence."

"I would only be a burden. I don't need her or anyone else. Just leave me alone. I'm a survivor. I think I proved that by surviving the plane crash, if that's what you want to call it. Now, go back to your home, Tina, and leave me be. I'll call you once I get back to my place. Thank you for coming, but it wasn't necessary. You have a family to take care of so you don't need a cripple to add to your duties."

"I think you need to add a psychologist to your convalescing period. You are alive and still in good physical shape; so, you are missing a part of your anatomy. Big deal. There are thousands of people who probably would wish they could be in your condition. Quit feeling sorry for yourself. Once you get that prosthesis, you'll be as good as new."

"It's easy for you to say. You have two legs and walk just fine."

"Once you get your new leg, you'll find that you also will walk just like you did before. That branch of the medical field has made great strides in having patients adapt to their new limbs. It's as if they had never lost them. You'll see. Have faith."

"Yeah, that faith thing bit me in the ass. My friend, from the plane crash, told me to have faith when I said I had just become engaged and was scared that I would never see Jane again. Look how that turned out."

"You can still have your Jane. It's you that's stopping that scene."

"Go home, Tina. I'm tired of arguing with you."

With that, she kissed him on the cheek and left. A while later Melina and Jean Claude came to visit.

Jean Claude said, "I understand you're going home in a few days. That's wonderful news."

"I see that you're doing much better. Did the doctors manage to get all of your organs back to where they should be?"

"Yes, they did; and my back is almost as good as new. They said that if Melina hadn't done what she did, I probably wouldn't be alive today."

Melina asked, "Have you talked to your fiancée?"

"I told you that I am no longer engaged and will never see Jane again. As far as she knows, I'm dead and I plan on keeping it that way; and so will you. Let's change the subject. So, you two are a couple now?"

Jean Claude took Melina's hand and grinned as they looked at Nick.

"You two lovebirds are so lucky. It could have been under much better circumstances that you met each other, but what does that matter. I remember when Jane and I first met. She and a friend were traveling through Florida and their boat died in some swamp land. Fortunately, I just happened to come along. That started an on-again-off-again relationship for many years until she proposed to me a few weeks ago. Life does take some drastic turns once in a while."

Melina said, "You can still have a wonderful life with her. You just need to quit feeling sorry for yourself. Thousands of people are in worse shape. Quit the pity party."

"My sister just left after giving me the same lecture and you know what I told her? GO HOME! I'm telling you two the same thing. GO HOME!"

Jean Claude said, "You can't get rid of us that easy. We all have a bond together for a lifetime. We will be by your side every step of the way, Nick. Surviving that plane crash was 100 times worse than your not having a part of your leg. We're a family and we'll help you overcome your bitterness and anger."

"Geee, my sister said I should hire a psychologist. Maybe I should just use the two of you."

"No sarcasm, please."

"Okay, okay. Jean Claude, you've been such a good friend in a very short time and I'll be forever grateful; and Melina, I may not have been alive today had it not been for your tending to me. When I arrived here at the hospital, I cursed you for many days having saved my life. I'm not ready to forgive you for that yet but am sure I will at some future point in time. Once I get back to my chalet in Italy and am mobile again with my prosthesis, I'll invite both of you to stay for a few days,weeks, or maybe even months."

Jean Claude said, "WOW, Melina. A few minutes ago he was kicking us out of here and now we have a full blown invitation to his beautiful home."

Nick responded, "I don't know how beautiful it is as I haven't been there for a few months but I do have plenty of room. It overlooks Lake Como; and it'll be fun to have us together in an actual home versus a converted plane wreck."

With that, they all laughed, hugged each other, and then the happy couple left.

Chapter Twenty One

The next morning, while the ladies were having breakfast, Jane said to Marie, "This is going to be one of our longer trips. Fortunately, we've been blessed with beautiful weather and we'll be traveling on I-70 most of the way so, hopefully, we'll have smooth sailing."

"Don't jinx us, Jane. So far there've been no breakdowns, other than me and your bump on the head. When you say a longer trip, how far is it?"

"Just a little over 200 miles, but we can pull over every two hours to stretch our legs. It's also good to make sure you don't get any blood clots."

"That's kind of you. Let's close up shop and hit the road."

While traveling Marie wanted to make sure Jane wasn't getting tired from driving, so she asked, "Some of the past few stops we've had, you mentioned such 'fun' things to do. So what do we have to look forward to on this next stop?"

"As I mentioned a few days ago, the highlight will be Arches National Monument. The campground has tours scheduled that will take us there and pick us up. They can't drive right up to Arches, but you should be okay. We can take another day and drive through Canyon lands national parks. I guess there are dramatic rock formations and all kinds of vistas. It'll be lots of fun and you won't have to walk much other than to Arches. Trust me, it'll be worth it."

"So far, this has been one of our most memorable trips; but then we always say that on every adventure that we pursue."

"You've got that right."

After the ladies found the campground and settled in at their site, they were sitting in their lounge chairs out on the patio. Jane fixed them some drinks and handed a bowl of peanuts to Marie. "I bought these hard-shelled peanuts at our last stop. We haven't munched on these in a long time." Just then, Jane's cell phone rang and she looked at the number hoping it was Nick but it was Frank.

"Hello, Frank. How's the packing going?"

"I've never had to do it as my wife always handled this part of the move. I cheated and hired a moving company to do it all. They are scheduled to come next Tuesday and will have all of it at my new place in Sacramento Friday afternoon. That's hitting right at the July 4 weekend so I'll have extra time to get settled. They're even going to unpack all of it for me too. It's pretty expensive to go that route but I won't have to worry about anything. I've spent the last few days going through all of the closets and getting rid of a lot of stuff. I've heard you say that one can never have enough stuff but I dispute that comment."

"Well, there are times when one needs to curb ones wants and needs. Did you buy a place in Sacramento or are you renting?"

"I don't want to buy anything until this home sells. There've been a few interested prospects so it should sell quickly. I also don't want to buy anything until I've lived there a while. I want to get a lay of the land, as they say."

"I guess that makes sense. When do you start at the hospital?"

"Boy, you ask a lot of questions. Actually, I don't start until the end of the month. I'm glad that I have the time as I'm struggling with all of these changes. I need to sit back and take a breath. I wish you could be with me now. You make me feel so relaxed and at peace with myself. You're a good friend, Jane."

"How can you say that? You've only been with me for a few hours."

"At our age, one knows when they feel comfortable with someone. Do you know yet when you will be getting to Sacramento?"

"Remember, Frank, that I'm engaged to be married."

"I remember. Have you heard from your fiancée?"

"No, but I will soon."

"Again I ask, when will you get to Sacramento?"

"We are still on schedule so right now it looks like July 16."

"That's perfect. I'll be anxiously awaiting your arrival."

"Chill, Frank. Have a good evening. Goodbye."

After Jane hung up, Marie wanted the loaded details. She said, "Jane, you need to curb this new relationship. How are you going to explain it to Nick when he comes back?"

"To begin with, I'm not in a relationship; and second, there's nothing to tell Nick, so quit worrying. We have a busy day tomorrow, so let's go in and get some rest."

Chapter Twenty Two

After the ladies toured Arches National Monument and drove through many scenic areas, they broke camp and were on their way to Provo, Utah. "I'm excited about going to our next campground," said Jane.

"That's good. So what do you have us doing?"

"For starters, I'm going to push you in a wheel chair on a 14 mile paved Provo River Trail."

"That's funny—you're pushing me for 14 miles. Why would you do such a thing?"

"From what I've read, there's beautiful scenery around every bend and I don't want you to miss it. Maybe we won't go the entire distance but I want to give it a try."

"We can start early in the morning and pack a lunch. I can also push myself for a while, at least until my hands get tired. This trip surely is different than our other ones, since it's really challenging us to be creative. Years from now, when we read our journals, I'll bet this will be one of the funniest ones."

"Let's get back to what we'll be doing. I've never been to the Sundance Ski Resort. I understand there is even horseback riding there; but we aren't going to tackle that again even if you wanted to give it a try."

"What do you mean, give it a try? Remember how I did on our trip through Kentucky? I even impressed the hired hands. That was so much fun as I hadn't been on a horse in years. If you'll recall, I did great riding the horse in Wyoming. It was you that had a problem."

"Yes, it was me; and I said that I wouldn't ride a horse again."

"On with what we'll be doing. I understand that there's a waterfall that plummets 607 feet to the Provo River. The campground directory says it's four miles up Provo Canyon. I sure hope we can see it from the road. After pushing you 14 miles, I don't know if I'll have the energy to push your wheelchair four miles up a canyon."

"You weren't exaggerating when you said there's lots to do. I hope we'll have some time to just relax and have our cocktails."

"We'll always find time to have our cocktails, Marie. Not to worry."

By the time the ladies finished their conversation, they had arrived at their next campground. As they turned into the area, they just couldn't get over the beauty. They were surrounded by mountains and their campsite was right by the river.

Jane said, "Out of all of the campgrounds that we've visited over the years, these last few out west have to be the best, but then I do love my mountains."

"I can see why. Every turn is breathtaking."

The ladies managed to conquer the entire 14 mile hiking trip but were exhausted when they returned to their campsite. They had taken lots of pictures and had acquired a few blisters along the way. "I think we should rest tomorrow, so we're all prepared for Sundance."

The following Tuesday, they headed for Sundance. Once they made it to the entrance, they then drove what seemed to be forever until they reached the main lodge. Jane said, "I knew I was going to be impressed, but this is much higher than my wildest expectations. Just look at the immense size of the range. It's like a hidden treasure among the mountains. Let's go shopping in those beautiful boutiques."

"Instead of shopping, let's go find the riding stables. This is really God's country and I'll bet we can find some fantastic vistas and summits while riding horses."

"You managed to get me to do that just recently and look how it turned out. Thanks, but no thanks."

"Well, I tried. You're going to have to push me in a wheelchair again."

"That's fine by me, as long as I don't have to get on a horse."

The ladies enjoyed their shopping and even visited some of the beautiful art galleries. "These paintings and sculptures are beautiful, don't you think so, Marie?"

"I agree. It's amazing to see such talent in one place. I understand that there is a famous art festival here every year."

"I'm getting hungry. Let's go try out one of the popular restaurants. I heard people talking about John's Bistro. Let's give it a whirl."

"Sounds like a plan."

The ladies feasted on some culinary tastes and then drove back to camp.

"I don't know about you, Marie, but I'm exhausted. These past few days have really done me in. By the way, how's the foot doing?"

"The wheelchair helps, but it's still swollen. I really need to be home lying on my couch being bored, but this is much more fun; and how's your head doing?"

"I haven't had any problems with it. Fortunately, I don't get sick very often and hardly ever have a headache. Let's get to bed early. Fortunately, we have only about 150 miles to drive tomorrow."

Chapter Twenty Three

Nick was terribly nervous about flying, so he made sure that the weather was going to be calm and clear the day of departure. The doctors gave him a prescription to help settle him and he popped four of them just before taking off. Fortunately, there was no turbulence and the plane arrived safely. Franceau was his physical therapist while in the hospital, so Nick offered him a good wage to work for him full time and Franceau accepted. Nick's maid was at the airport to get them. It was a nice warm summer day and Nick was feeling much better both physically and mentally.

Once they arrived at the chateau, Franceau helped Nick get into his wheelchair. Franceau said, "If you continue to improve as you have been doing, you'll be back to your old self in no time at all."

"Both you and I know that's never going to happen as you have two good legs and I'm a cripple."

"They're almost finished fitting that titanium leg of yours and it will be almost like your other one."

"Yeah, sure. I know there are many who have artificial legs and act perfectly normal, but people can be mean. I can picture myself walking down a street and looking at others around me. Just for fun, I would pull up my pant leg and they would all gasp and walk away from me, like I'm a freak."

"Society has come a long way in acceptance of people with disabilities. How about that guy who raced in the Olympics? He doesn't feel sorry for himself."

"It may look like that in public but you can't convince me that he doesn't sit in his home at times and feel depressed."

"Maybe so, but all of us are depressed at one time or another. You need acceptance, Nick, before you can move on with your life."

"Yeah, this is some life. I've lost the only person who meant anything to me, so I have nothing."

"You can't say that this beautiful chateau overlooking Lake Como is nothing. Then there's your sister, her children, Gabritta, Jean Claude and Melina. I would be privileged to also be considered your friend. And your talking about losing the only person that mattered, I believe that was your choice to end it."

"Let's change the subject. I'm tired and going to rest for a while."

"I think we should do some exercises first. You were sitting a long time and we need to get that blood flowing."

"Okay, but go easy on me. You can be mean tomorrow. I don't want to fire you on your first day."

"That's kind of you."

"If you would, tell Gabritta to prepare a light dinner this evening. We'll dine at 8:00PM."

"That sounds fancy. Do we dress formal?"

"Of course not."

The following day, Franceau got word that Nick's leg was ready for fitting. The specialist came to the chateau and was pleased at how it fit just below the knee. "Let's see you walk with it, Nick."

Nick was pleasantly surprised at how light it was and easy to maneuver. "I have to admit that I wasn't thrilled at the prospect of having something foreign on me, but this thing isn't half bad."

Franceau said, "I'm proud of you, Nick. You may not need me to be around for very long."

"You're wrong on that score, Franceau. Once this therapy thing is finished, I have other plans for you, but only if you agree."

"That depends on what type of plans."

"Let's discuss it after the specialist leaves."

Chapter Twenty Four

As the ladies traveled along I-80, Jane said, "We have three stops through Nevada, but they don't sound exciting. We'll be driving pretty much through the plains and we might see wild mustangs. That would be an awesome sight. I read in the directory that the world-famous Bonneville Salt Flats is only ten miles away from our next campground. It's used for setting records with customized cars. That would be a good bucket-list item for me to ride in one of those cars. You know how much I love to go fast."

"Yes, I do. Sometimes I get nervous when you get a lead foot. It's a wonder you don't get more speeding tickets."

"I try to go with the flow of traffic. Very seldom do I go over the speed limit, if there's no one in front of me."

"You are a very cautious driver, Jane. That's why I always feel safe and secure with your driving. It's a good thing, as I don't like to drive much anymore with my poor eyesight."

As they were driving along, Marie's cell phone rang. It was Vince who said that he was back at the ranch. "When will you be home, Marie? I miss you terribly."

"We're on our way right now heading for Wendover, Nevada and are right on schedule. Barring any mishaps, we should be home around mid August, just as we had planned."

"I believe you've already had some mishaps. Your tripping and hurting your foot, plus Jane getting hit in the head could be called mishaps."

"I meant those that mess up our schedule, like the truck breaking down or the RV doing some kooky thing."

"Well, I certainly hope that nothing like that is going to happen. Let's change the subject. I don't have any further news to report regarding Nick's being alive. It doesn't look good, Marie."

"I know. Jane hasn't had any word either. We're just pulling into the campground, sweetheart, so I will close. I miss you. Goodbye."

"Jane asked, "I assume that was Vince. Did he say anything about Nick?"

"I'm afraid there's no further information; but don't give up hope."

"I never will until someone gives me concrete evidence to the contrary. Nick is still alive."

"That-a-girl!"

They checked in at the camp office and then found their site.

They spent the afternoon relaxing in their lounge chairs and reading their books. Jane said, "Would you mind if we just relax this weekend? I would like to see the Bonneville Salt Flats; but I'd also like one day where we don't have to get in the truck."

"I agree. That's fine with me. I suppose we could try our hand at gambling. We could find a casino just about anyplace in Nevada."

"Gambling is not my cup of tea. I guess I'm not a risk taker."

"I don't know about that. You've done some pretty risky things in the past few years."

"Yes, but not with my money. That's probably why I'm not rich. Nick likes to play the stock market and he's pretty good at it. I have no idea how the bond market or mutual funds work. At this stage of my life, it's probably too late to try."

"My motto is, that it's never too late to try anything. Just look at us. We're two old broads still traveling and exploring. We may get hurt along the way, but we certainly do have fun, Don't we?"

"Yes, we do, Marie."

That evening, Frank called Jane to report that he had settled into his new apartment. "I haven't lived in an apartment in many years. This is a new experience and kinda fun. No worries about things breaking down and no maintaining of stuff. You can leave your worries behind, as they say. In fact, my home in Gothenburg just sold, so I don't even have to worry about that."

"It sounds like you are well on your way to a new chapter in your life."

"That's true and I'd love to have you in it. I realize that we'd only be friends and I can accept that."

"You're a great guy, Frank, but you need to find someone who will be your soul mate."

"I've already found her, but she seems to be attached to someone else. That's okay. On another matter, are you still scheduled to get here July 16?"

"It looks more like July 17. Right now we're in Wendover, Nevada. Marie still has her gimpy foot and I had an altercation in Cheyenne while riding a horse."

"You rode a horse? I thought you told me that you don't like to ride."

"I don't but we can't do any hiking with Marie's foot, so I broke down and rode. As we were going down a trail, I was looking at Marie and my head caught a limb. Down I went and it even knocked me out. I had a slight concussion, but quickly mended."

"I don't picture you being a clumsy one."

"I'm not usually. I blamed it on the horse."

Frank chuckled over that comment and then said, "Before I forget, please write down my address so you know exactly where to go when you arrive in Sacramento. This complex has a large parking area and I already checked with the office as to where you can park that big rig of yours."

"That's very gracious of you. Please thank them for me. We have a full schedule tomorrow, so I'd better get some sleep. Have a good evening, Frank. Goodbye."

After Jane ended the call, she told Marie that Frank found a place to park their rig once they arrived in Sacramento.

"Do you mean that we'll be staying in a parking lot for days on end instead of a campground? I DON'T THINK SO!"

"No. It's just overnight. Frank's apartment is near his hospital, which also is near the state capitol; and our campground is also near the state capitol."

"Then why don't we just go to the campground and then you can go see your Frank once we unhook and set up?"

"To begin with, he's not my Frank. I'm still engaged, remember? Secondly, I thought it would save us one night of expense."

"Ohhh, sure. We're so broke that we can't afford a $30-$40 camping fee."

"Enough, Marie. We're just friends. Besides, he can take a look at your foot to see how it's doing."

"My foot is just fine. I think you're getting into dangerous waters and might not get out without someone getting hurt. In fact, it could end up being all three of you and no one being happy."

"Frank is good for me right now. I've never loved anyone as much as I love Nick. That will never change. It's so easy to talk to Frank and he makes me feel safe."

"Just remember this conversation when Nick comes back."

"Let's get to bed."

The next day the ladies drove through the salt flats and felt like they could see for miles. "This is really desolate and barren. "I hope the truck doesn't break down," said Marie.

"Don't jinx us. We've been doing just fine. I do think we'd better get back to the campground though, as we have about 240 miles to travel Monday; and I'd like to stay out of this truck tomorrow."

Chapter Twenty Five

The following Monday, the ladies drove across Nevada and made it safely to Winnemucca, Nevada, late that afternoon. They couldn't find a campground so decided to spend the night in a shopping plaza parking lot area that was marked for campers and truckers. As they pulled into the plaza, they parked by another RV. "I'll agree to this, Jane, but pray we don't have an experience like we did many months ago in another shopping plaza parking lot. Remember when someone tried to break in and you threatened them with your shotgun that you didn't have?"

"Yes, I remember; and you made me promise that we'd never stay in one of these places again. However, there are two other RVs here, plus three trucks and plenty of parking lot lights. I think we'll be fine."

They got out of the truck and Jane put blocks under the tires. "We have a full tank of water and the sewer box is empty so we should be fine. Just take it easy on the resources."

"Yes, mam. Do you think there are any Indian reservations around here?"

"That's a strange question. Would you think the name of the town would be a clue? I'm sure if we researched it, we would find some interesting facts and history. Since I didn't unhook the truck and we can't go anyplace, why don't you research it on the computer while I journal. We've got a lot of catching up to do in our journal."

The ladies spent the evening relaxing and watching some videos on their big-screen television. Jane was looking at the itinerary. "Our next stop is Reno, Nevada. The directory says that the campground has a 24-hour shuttle to Boomtown. I've never been there and assume that it's a gambling and entertainment place."

"Geee, that's what both of us like to do—NOT! Is there anything else; and how long do you have us staying at that swinging place?"

"Well, we can take a riding tour of the scenic Truckee River and surrounding mountains. Nearby is a sporting good retail store and mini-mart, At least that's what the directory says."

"WOW, you really know how to get me excited!"

"I told you a few days ago, that there wouldn't be a lot to do along this corridor. At least, nothing that we like to do. We can't be doing all kinds of fun stuff every single day. Our old bones can't take it anymore; and besides, you're supposed to stay off of that foot."

"My foot is healing more and more every day. In fact, I'm ready to take of this terrible boot."

"It's only been one month and Frank said you should wait until you get back home and have your doctor look at it."

"Since we'll be in Sacramento in a few days, I'll just have Frank look at it again. Hopefully, he'll let me take it off."

"That'll work. Let's get some sleep."

"I'll try, but I'm not comfortable knowing we're in a parking lot, where we can get mugged."

"We're not going to get mugged. Would you rather we take shifts and guard our quarters?"

"No, thank you. I remember that time we camped in the Alleghany Mountains and took two hour shifts stoking that small fireplace stove for heat. That sure was a FUN time!"

"Yes, we do have some great memories, don't we."

The ladies did their stint in Reno and moved on to Sacramento. They arrived in early afternoon; and Jane had Marie call Frank. "Frank, this is Marie. We are presently on Business Loop 80 west heading to Enterprise Blvd. Are we near you?"

"Yes, you are. Put your phone on speaker and I'll direct you. You're only a few blocks away."

The ladies managed to get that big rig through a congested area and some streets were very narrow. Of course, Jane was laughing again. Once they arrived at the complex, there was Frank standing at the entrance. He directed them to the area where the office said to park. Jane had no trouble because, fortunately, it was a pull-through area. Jane put blocks under the RV and truck.

Frank said, "I don't think I ever saw your RV before. This thing is huge; and take a look at that truck. You don't look like the type to be driving a diesel truck, Jane."

"Actually, my only experience has been driving cars. I did drive a van once, but that's it. I've owned Lincolns for many years. When Marie and I decided to do this traveling thing, I traded my two-year old

Lincoln for a Ford F350 turbo diesel 4X4. I love it when I come out of a store and the guys are going goo-goo eyed over my truck. I walk up to it and say, 'do you like my truck, guys?' You should see the look on their faces."

"I can see why they would be surprised. I'm impressed. How long is that 5th wheel anyhow? About 40'?"

"You're close. It's really only 38'."

"Excuse me? Only 38'? WOW. Now, I'm really impressed!"

Frank told them that the complex helped a local paving company park their big rigs in exchange for free paving. "That's why there's so much of an area reserved for large vehicles. Let's go up to my apartment. I'm sure you two are exhausted. I have your favorite Scotch and I also made a pu-pu platter."

Marie couldn't get over how he remembered their talking about a pu-pu platter.

As they strolled through the complex, the ladies were impressed at the size and beautiful condition of the grounds. They walked through some tropical landscaping and passed a three-tiered fountain.

"This is impressive," said Jane.

"Yes, I'm glad that they had an apartment available. With the hospital so close, I guess they get a lot of nurses and doctors. I've already met some that I'll be working with. Every day I'm more and more comfortable having made the right decision."

"I'm so happy for you, Frank."

Once inside the apartment, Frank looked at Marie's foot. "Your foot looks like it's healing nicely, Marie. You've done a good job with the convalescence. If you don't mind, I'd like to take you to the hospital tomorrow and get it x-rayed. Maybe you can then take that walking cast off."

"That's music to my ears. Thank you."

"Don't thank me yet. We have to look at the x-rays first."

"Yes, doctor."

After they took a tour of the apartment, they went out to the balcony and Frank started the propane fireplace.

Marie said, "This place must be costing you a fortune, Frank." Jane quietly scolded her for making that comment.

Frank said, "That's okay, Jane. Actually, the hospital gets quite a deal as they want their doctors and nurses to live close by. Once I start working, many times I'll do 24-hour shifts. I'll also be on call a lot, so the hospital wants to keep the complex happy. That goes vice versa also, for the complex keeping the hospital happy. I guess it's a win win for all sides."

Later that evening Frank prepared steaks on the grill while the ladies poured wine. When they went inside, Frank told them that they each could have a bedroom and he would sleep on the couch. Marie said, "I don't know about Jane, but I'm going to sleep in my own bed out in the RV. In fact, if you don't mind, I'll freshen up in the guest bathroom and head for that comfy bed of mine now. My foot is hurting and I'm tired."

Jane said, "I'll come with you, Marie."

"That's not necessary. This place is well lighted and I saw security cameras everywhere. I'm sure it's quite safe. You two go out and enjoy that nice fireplace. I'll be fine."

Frank walked Marie to the door and kissed her on the cheek. He reminded her to keep her cell phone close and to call him at any hour if she needed anything. Then he and Jane went back out to the balcony.

After a while Jane told him that she needed to go back to the RV. "Please stay here, Jane. I've missed you so much and I don't want you to leave."

"I keep reminding you that I'm engaged; and we don't need to have this relationship go to the next step."

"I know. I keep telling myself that, but what happens if Nick never comes back." Before Jane could respond, he kissed her softly on the lips. She started to pull away, but enjoyed it so much that she kissed him back. After a long kiss and some fondling, they sat back and just stared at each other.

"This is not a good situation, Frank. You need to get involved at the hospital and meet another doctor or nurse. Forget me as I'll only be trouble for you."

"I don't want to meet anyone else. Please spend the night with me."

"I can't do that. I'm leaving now. I don't want to see you anymore and please don't call me. Marie and I will be gone in the morning. Goodbye." As she left, she had tears in her eyes.

When Jane went inside the RV, Marie was still awake and saw that Jane had been crying. "Are you okay?"

"I don't think so, but I'll get better."

"Do you want to talk about it?"

"Not really. Let's go to sleep. We're leaving early in the morning. In fact, if you don't mind, I'd like to leave here and go to our next stop. It's in Visalia, CA and 240 miles away. I need to get far away from here."

"Did you do something with Frank that you're going to regret?"

"No, but if we don't leave, I'm sure it could reach that point. I'm still convinced that Nick is alive and I want my one and only love to come back to me."

"I agree that we should leave. We had visited this area two years ago and never saw Visalia so let's get moving. We can even stay there for more than a few days. It'll give us both some time to relax and rewind."

"Good idea, Marie. I really need to do some reflecting of my life."

Chapter Twenty Six

The ladies made it to Visalia by early afternoon. Once they unhooked and had their chairs set out, Marie said she would fix them a drink. "Make mine a tall and strong one, Marie. I want to collapse and think of nothing but having fun in this beautiful area."

"You're on, sister."

While Marie was inside fixing drinks, Vince called. "Marie, I have something to tell you. Is Jane nearby?"

"No, I'm inside fixing drinks and she's outside working on a fire."

"Good. I just found out some shocking news and you may have a difficult time telling Jane."

"You have news about Nick? Is he gone?"

"No, he's alive and was found at the same time as the others."

"But that doesn't make sense. The news media said only three people were found."

"I know. Nick paid a lot of money to keep it that way. He even changed his name to Nicholas Cambini. You see, he lost part of his leg and didn't want Jane to know. He feels like an invalid and didn't want to be a burden to Jane. He even set up a trust fund for her. I found this out last week when he called and explained the turn of events. He wants me to secretly give Jane money on a monthly basis. I told him that I wouldn't do that as he needs to come back to the USA and face Jane himself. He got angry with me and hung up."

"Where is Nick now?"

"He's been at his chateau in Italy since he was released from the hospital. I guess he hired his physical therapist, from the hospital, full time."

"This is all too shocking to take in at one time. I don't have any idea how to approach Jane with this information."

"I told you it would be difficult."

"Do you remember my doctor from Gothenburg, Nebraska?"

"The one you accused me of being jealous?"

"Yes. Well, he has the biggest crush on Jane. In fact, he took a job in Sacramento. We just left there yesterday as something happened between the two of them and Jane wouldn't tell me. She's been sobbing ever since. I can't give her this information now. She's not in any shape to deal with it. I'm having a hard time dealing with it."

"You've had a lot of psychology classes, so I'll trust your judgment on dealing with it. Good luck."

"Thanks. Please keep this quiet for now. I'll tell her in a day or two."

"I wish I could be there when you tell her. In fact, I think I'll fly into LAX tomorrow. My business is in between clients and I have the time. Can you pick me up at the airport?"

"Ohhh, my. That would be wonderful, sweetheart. Just let me know the time. There's no way I could explain to Jane why I would need the truck, so I think I'll just say we miss each other too much and couldn't wait another day. That's no lie, either."

Marie took the drinks outside and acted so excited. "What's going on, Marie? Your expression looks like you swallowed the canary."

I just got off the phone with Vince. He's back from his business trips and can't wait until mid August to see me. Would you mind driving me to the airport in Los Angeles tomorrow? He's flying here. Isn't that wonderful news?"

"Sure. I'm happy for you."

"That didn't sound very convincing. I'm sorry, Jane. You seem to have two loves in your life and can't have either one of them."

"I have only one love being Nicholas Camboli and I will be with him soon. Are you aware that LAX is about 200 miles from here?"

"I thought the directory said that this campground is halfway between San Francisco and Los Angeles."

"It is, but the distance between those two is 400 miles. Our next stop was going to be Barstow. It's also 200 miles but takes us further east. We were going to stay in Sacramento for seven days. Since we didn't do that, how about we go to the campground in Acton, CA. It's about 180 miles south but then we'll be about 40 miles from the airport. If we get up very early tomorrow, and I mean about 5:30AM, we could be on the road by 7:00AM. This would put us in Acton around 11:00-11:30 barring no stopping. When does Vince's plane arrive?"

"He hasn't made the reservation yet. We were just chatting and saying how much we missed each other; and then I felt the light bulb flash in his eyes. That's when he said he would fly here."

"Call him back and tell him our plans. Have him arrive no earlier than 3:00. By the time we get to the campground and unhook, we'll need to rest a bit. We can take I-405 directly to the airport, but LA is a nightmare to drive, no matter the time of day. It can take us one-three hours and I'm not exaggerating."

"I really appreciate this, Jane. I can only imagine how much you miss Nick. He will come back to you. I know he will."

"Of course he will. If we're getting up so early, let's tear down as much as we can tonight. In fact, let's hook up Maynard to Willie.** Hopefully, it'll go smoothly. We've been pretty lucky lately with the hooking up and unhooking. Remember how frustrated I would get when we first started traveling?"

"Yes, I do; but once you learned all of the tricks, it's really been going smoothly."

"The land underneath plays a big part. I always love it when we have a concrete pad. On slag, I would have to pull the truck forward a little, raise the hitch a little, or back up a little and lower the hitch a little. That was a big pain."

"And when all else failed, you would have WD40 to the rescue."

"That stuff always works miracles."

**Footnote: In the first book, the ladies named their truck Maynard and the 5th wheel was named Willie.

Marie's cell phone rang and it was Vince telling her that his plane would be arriving at 3:55PM. She let him know that they were going to be in Acton around noon. She told Jane the time of the plane's arrival."

"I hope it will be on time. LA is crazy in the off hours, let alone driving at rush hour. Probably, what we should do, is pick Vince up at the airport and then go someplace close for dinner instead of going directly back to the campground. In that way, maybe we'll divert the rush hour."

"Good plan. Let's get moving lady. I'm anxious to see my honey."

Chapter Twenty Seven

Franceau said, "I'm interested in hearing what plans you have for me, Nick. Over the last few weeks, you and I have bonded. We've learned a lot about each other. As you know, I'm an only child and my parents will killed in a car crash when I was only 23 years old. I've had some serious relationships the past few years, but none lasted. My work has been my life, but I'm beginning to wonder if there's not something else for me."

"I'm glad to hear that. I have a male assistant in the states who's been helping me with my businesses. In fact, he takes care of my home in Florida. I would like to set up a structure whereby he continues to manage the businesses that are in the states; and, if you're interested, you would manage those here across Europe. I can have him come here and he can explain to you what he does for me. From there, you can decide if that would be of interest to you; and I certainly hope that it will."

"First, can you give me a little insight into exactly what type of businesses we are talking about. I'm assuming that they are all legitimate. How many are we talking about?"

"I dabble in the stocks and bonds market. There are also some real estate holdings."

"Sounds fascinating, but you're assuming that I have some expertise in these fields. As far as you know, I'm just a physical therapist."

"I can read into people pretty well. You and I have spent a lot of time together these past weeks. I have every confidence that you would be a good fit."

"Then, let's see what your assistant has in store for me. I'm also assuming that you've already discussed this strategy with him."

"Most assuredly. In fact, he's been saying for quite some time that the work load has grown to such a size, that we need more help; so, he's excited to bring you on board."

Nick's assistant, James, arrived a few days later. He and Franceau worked closely with Nick. As the days went by, Franceau was getting into the groove. "I'm so blessed to have met you, Nick. I really think this new position will work. It's very intriguing. You have a lot of businesses. I never realized how wealthy you are."

"Money isn't everything, Franceau. I would give it all up if I could have my natural leg back and be with Jane."

"Technically, you do have your leg back and you could be with Jane."

"You harp just like all of the others. Why don't any of you understand how I feel about this thing?"

James said, "I'm sure, if Jane were here, you wouldn't even notice that you had an artificial limb. You've adjusted to it beautifully. When you wear slacks, no one would even know that it's not the real thing.

You have no limp and you motor around this place like you're a teenager. GET OVER IT AND CALL HER."

Nick stared at the two of them for a moment and then said, "I'm leaving you two here in the office; and I'm going for a walk."

Franceau looked at James and said, "Did you hear that James? He's going for a walk."

"Yes, I did. That's wonderful. Take your time, Nick. I do think that I'll check with Gabritta though to see when she's planning dinner. I'm really enjoying her Italian dishes. If I don't leave soon, I'll be a lot heavier than I already am."

While Nick went for his walk, Franceau asked James, "Nick's mentioned a close friend in the states by the name of Vince. What if you were to call him and tell him that Nick is actually alive."

"To be quite frank with you, Nick called him last week as he had me set up a trust fund for Jane. Nick asked Vince to be the one to discreetly give it to her on a monthly basis and Vince refused. I guess he told Nick to go back to the states and give it to her himself. Nick got angry and hung up on him."

"That's why he was so moody. I couldn't get him to exercise at all for a few days. Now I understand. His going for a walk today was shocking but wonderful. He needs to do that every day."

"I believe we're making progress. We'll get him and Jane back together yet."

While Nick was on his walk, he called Jean Claude. "Do you and Melina have any plans this week? I really miss you two."

"We were just talking about you last night and how you had promised us an invitation to your home. We were beginning to wonder if you had forgotten us."

"That would never happen. Get your plane tickets and let Franceau know when you'll arrive so he can pick you up at the airport."

"I thought Franceau was your therapist."

"He has been; but since I have this new thing stuck to my leg, I'm pretty mobile. In fact, I'm out here going for a walk alone and it feels wonderful."

"I don't know if I ever heard you say that word 'wonderful' since I've known you."

"Well, don't get too excited. I'm still my grouchy self, especially if you two harp on that Jane thing again."

"So, why would a therapist be a chauffeur?"

"Actually, Franceau agreed to take over many duties that my assistant from the states does. Since I'm going to stay in Italy permanently, I need an assistant to help me with the European accounts. It's just too difficult to have James perform those duties from the states. I'm still keeping him on the payroll as I have a few businesses in the states and he takes care of my home in Florida."

"You're a fascinating man Mr. Camboli."

"I'm Nicholas Cambini now, remember?"

"Okay, Nick. Whatever you say. Let me talk to Melina and we'll let Franceau know our plans. Take care of yourself. It'll be fun to just sit around a beautiful chateau and talk about old times."

"I don't know how much fun that would be but I'm anxious to see the two of you. Give Melina my best. See you soon."

The following Wednesday, Franceau went to the airport to get Jean Claude and Melina. While driving back to the chateau, Jean Claude asked Franceau, "Be honest and tell us exactly how Nick is doing. We are so concerned about his mental attitude and adjusting to his new way of doing things."

"Nick's come a long way from when I first met him. If you'll recall, he didn't want to live. At least I haven't heard him say that for a while. In fact, he went for a walk by himself for the first time the other day and on his own initiative. James and I were pleasantly surprised but then we probably had something to do with that motivation."

Melina asked, "What do you mean?"

"We were discussing his businesses. I didn't realize how many he had so I made a comment about how wealthy he must be. His response was that he'd give it all up if he could have his natural leg back and be with Jane. I said that he has the next best thing with the artificial leg and it's his choice not to have Jane. That's when he stormed out of the house."

"I guess we still have a lot of work to do on that man, Jean Claude. Has anyone tried contacting Jane?"

Franceau responded, "I think that would be a huge mistake at this point in time. Nick contacted his best friend from the states the other day. At first, I thought that was wonderful progress as he had been acting as if he had never even been to the states; but then I discovered why he had called. He wants James and me to set up a monthly trust fund for Jane and he called Vince to be the go between. Vince refused and told him to go see Jane himself and give it to her personally.

Nick got very angry and hung up on him. Boy, was he ever moody after that conversation."

Jean Claude said, "I'll bet Nick's friend was shocked at that phone call as he probably thought Nick was killed in the plane crash. This is such a sad situation. Nick loves Jane so much; and from what I've surmised, Jane is probably dying from a broken heart. Surely, there's something that we can do. How about we talk to this Vince fellow and get his take on the matter?"

"Good idea. Here's my cell phone with Vince's number in it. Please call him now while we're driving back to the chateau."

Jean Claude dialed the number and explained his relationship with Nick. Vince was pleased to hear from him. Vince told him that he was on his way to see his wife and Jane. "I don't know how much you know about Jane, but she and my wife travel a lot in a recreational vehicle. In fact, right now they're in Los Angeles. I called my wife and told her about my conversation with Nick. Needless to say, she was shocked as she and I both thought that Nick was killed in the plane crash. Of course, Jane keeps saying that he had gone down the mountain to find help and was still alive. My wife, Marie, didn't know how to approach Jane regarding the current situation; so I'm flying to Los Angeles to help her with the news."

"I don't envy you with that task. Is there some way we can help?"

"As a matter of fact, if you don't mind, I'd like to put you on the speaker phone after we've told Jane that Nick is alive. I'm sure she'll be ecstatic and want to go and see him. You can explain his mental attitude and how that wouldn't be a good idea just yet. I know Jane and she'll probably want to do it anyhow."

"We're heading for Nick's chateau right now. If you call and we're with him, I'll pretend that you're someone else and say, 'I don't think that's a good idea. Let me call you later.' That way, I can go to another part of the house and call you back."

"That should work. I'm so grateful that you called. If we put all of our minds together, we can get these two lovebirds back together again."

Jean Claude disconnected the call and noticed that they were riding along Lake Como. He said to Melina, "Man, this is really beautiful. I've never been to Italy. Just look at those homes, Melina. I guess that's a wrong term, when it looks like there's 100 or more rooms in them."

Franceau chimed in, "Just wait until you see Nick's Chateau. It'll take days for you to experience the grounds, the vineyards and the chateau, itself."

Both Jean Claude and Melina said together, "We can hardly wait!"

Chapter Twenty Eight

The next day the ladies were up bright and early and on their way to the town of Acton, CA. They made good time and pulled into the campground a little after 11:00. While they were resting, Jane was reading the directory. "It says here that we can see and do all sorts of stuff."

"I hope so. Vince and I have never visited California together. This will be fun. Just what stuff do you have in mind?"

"Since you decided to take that walking cast off by yourself, we can test that mended foot on the Pacific Crest Trail."

"That sounds cool, but I didn't think we were within a short walking distance to the Pacific Coast."

"We aren't. I said Pacific Crest. Tricky, huh. Anyhow, we can visit the theme parks and museums. If Vince doesn't want to do that, we can just sample all of the many restaurants in the area."

"Sounds like a plan; but, would you mind if we get going? I'm anxious to see my sweetheart and don't want to be late. You said LA traffic is a nightmare and I don't want to be stranded someplace and have him waiting at the airport."

"I don't mind at all; and can understand why you're anxious. I can't wait to see my sweetheart."

The ladies headed for LAX Airport and arrived just a few minutes before Vince's plane arrived. They were waiting in the main terminal and Marie said, "I can understand why they don't allow visitors to the gates anymore; but it's so confusing to try and find those that one needs to meet."

"I agree; and especially when one is in a huge terminal such as this one. Thankfully, they invented the cell phone. Did you tell Vince to call once he landed?"

"Yes, I did;" and then Marie's cell phone rang. "Timing is everything." Marie told Vince where they were located and a short time later he came into view. Marie ran to him and kissed him so hard that he almost fell over. "Boy, Marie, I don't ever remember you being so expressive. That was some kiss."

"I guess with Jane's being so concerned over whether Nick is alive or dead, I subconsciously want to make sure you understand how much you mean to me."

"That's reassuring, Marie. I promise that I'm not going anywhere and will always be by your side."

"Yeah. That's what Nick said and look what happened to him."

They walked back to where Jane was standing and she greeted Vince with a kiss on the cheek. Marie said, "Wait a minute, Jane, he's mine." Jane started crying and Marie hugged her. "I was only kidding, Jane. I'm so sorry."

"That's okay, Marie. I just get emotional when I see you two so happy and it makes me think of how much I miss my Nick."

Vince thought, *Jane is in more of an emotional, mental state than I had realized. I hope Marie and I can say the right words to give her comfort.*

Jane asked if they needed to go to the baggage claim to get his suitcase. "No, I just packed an overnight bag as I can't stay long. I just came for a few hours to see my sweetheart. My plane leaves tomorrow morning at 11:35AM."

"Then we had better get moving. Marie and I talked about finding a nice restaurant in the area so we don't hit rush hour traffic."

"I know just the place. It's pretty close and they have great food. Some of us ate there when we had a business conference out here."

Jane said, "That's great. Do you want to drive us there?"

"No, that's quite all right. I'll just hug my sweetheart and give you directions along the way. It's pretty easy to find."

Once they arrived at the restaurant, the parking attendant was in awe at the immense size of their beautiful truck. He gave Jane the ticket and she said to take good care of her baby. He just looked at her and grinned.

Once inside, Vince asked if they could have a table out in the courtyard. "Of course," was the answer. The three of them were led to a table in a tropical-like garden. It had little white lights in all of the trees. There were all types of flowers growing such as Birds of Paradise, Anthurium and Lava Plants. "Look Marie, at the White Dendrobiums. Aren't they beautiful?"

"I'm assuming that's a flower; and yes, they are beautiful. I'll bet Nick doesn't have these growing at his chateau in Italy."

"While that's true, he may have some of them at his place in Florida."

Once they were seated, Vince and Marie ordered drinks. Jane said, "I'll be the designated driver since no one else wants to drive my truck."

Marie said, "You can have just one. That shouldn't go over the limit."

Vince said, "I don't know about that, Marie. Many states now have zero tolerance."

Jane told them that they should just order and forget the debate about her drinking. Once they were finished with the fabulous meal and they all ordered dessert, Vince decided to start the dreaded conversation. "Jane, there was more than one reason why I wanted to fly here today. Please brace yourself for what I'm about to say and don't get impulsive."

"DID THEY FIND NICK DEAD????"

"Not at all."

"Then what are you trying to say? Talk to me."

"I'm trying." Marie intervened and told Jane to please be quiet and listen.

"I received a telephone call from Nick the other day asking me to secretly give you a monthly trust fund that he has set up for you. I told him to come back to the states and give it to you himself. He started yelling at me and then hung up."

"She started yelling, Nick doesn't yell; and why would he give me the money. Where is he? Is he injured? Why won't he call me? I want to go to him."

She was shaking and then started sobbing. Marie walked around the table and started to hug her.

She stopped sobbing and said, "I'm fine. Go sit down, Marie."

Vince proceeded to tell her that he had chatted with a couple who were with Nick after the plane crashed and they became good friends. "Their names are Jean Claude and Melina. In fact, they would like to talk to you about Nick's condition and how he is dealing with what has happened; but you need to stay calm, Jane. PLEASE, listen to them and wait until they are finished before asking questions. Can you do that?"

"Let me get my bearings first. I knew all along that he was alive, but I couldn't understand why he wouldn't call me. I'll listen to these people and will try to make sense of the conversation. I have a strange feeling that all of you are hiding something from me; and you're going to tell me that I shouldn't go to his place in Italy. At least, I'm assuming that's where he is. Just call them and let's get this out of the way."

"I do want to tell you first, that Melina is a registered nurse and saved both Jean Claude and Nick." Vince dialed Jean Claude's number and he said, "I'll call you later."

Vince told Jane that Jean Claude would say that if they were with Nick in his chateau. "That would be Jean Claude's signal that he needed a chance to go to the other end of the chateau for privacy."

Once Jean Claude called back and they were on speaker, he and Melina explained the turn of events. Melina told Jane, "I know you want to be with Nick, but he doesn't want you to see him. He is ashamed of his body and doesn't want to be a burden to you. PLEASE, give him time to adjust to his new leg. His mental state has improved immensely; but, at first, he just wanted to die. In fact, there was a period of time that he hated me for saving his life. He pulled a lot of strings to make it look like he was dead. The truth is, that he has even changed his name to Nicholas Cambini. Jean Claude and I have talked to Nick's sister and physical therapist. We all feel, that if you come to Italy now, it may push Nick further away from you. We all know that he loves you terribly, but he's still in denial and ashamed of his new body. You need to give him time to adjust."

"How much time are you talking about—a week, a month, a year, forever???"

"Vince tells us that you ladies are traveling out west. When do you plan on returning to your homes?"

"We originally planned to be back at Vince and Marie's in New Mexico in mid August but due to a change of events, it now looks like the beginning of August."

Melina said, "I don't think that would be enough time. We've been working on Nick to call you, as he is miserable without you. I know this is a very difficult situation for you; but, if it's not handled properly, you can push him away forever. I'm sure you don't want that to happen."

"That's for sure, but I'm also miserable without him. I'll wait until I get back to Ohio. Once I arrive there, I can't promise how much longer I will wait."

"Fair enough." They thanked everyone for their patience and understanding. Vince thanked Jean

Claude and Melina personally for all that they had done and are doing for Nick. Jane responded a big ditto, but was spent and sobbing again. Jean Claude gave Jane his cell phone number and told her that she could call him if she hadn't heard from him in a week. "I'll keep you updated as I receive information, but please don't call the chateau. It will only make a bad situation worse."

After the call was disconnected, Jane called the waiter over to their table and ordered a double Scotch on the rocks. "We may need to stay in a hotel for the night, but I want to have this drink."

"That's understandable," was a reply from both Vince and Marie.

A four piece band arrived over in one corner of the courtyard and started playing soft-rock music. Vince and Marie asked Jane if she minded their going out on the small dance floor. "Of course not," was the answer. "You two enjoy yourselves. I'll just sit here, try to digest all of the information that I've just received, and enjoy my Scotch."

Later that evening, Jane told them that they should stay at the hotel by the airport for the night. "I'll drop you two lovebirds off and I'll go back to our RV. You'll have much more privacy and I really would like to be alone to meditate."

Marie asked, "Will you be all right driving back by yourself?"

"I'm fine. I've already had three cups of coffee and went walking while you were dancing. You can get a cab in the morning and take Vince to the airport. I believe Vince said his plane was departing at 11:35AM. Is that right, Vince?"

"Yes, that's right; but are you sure you'll be okay, Jane?"

"I'm fine. I'll come back in the morning for you, Marie. This is best for all of us."

She took them to the hotel and kissed Vince on the cheek and then said, "I know it was hard for you to not comply with Nick's wishes, especially when you were relieved that he was okay. You're a good friend, Vince, and he'll recognize someday why you did what you did. I also appreciate your being here to support Marie when you gave me the news."

Jane bid them goodbye and then drove back to the campground. She made good time due to the late hour of the night.

Chapter Twenty Nine

Jane had a very restless night. She didn't understand why Nick wanted to keep his disability from her. She wouldn't have reacted that way if it had happened to her, or would she. *I suppose one never knows how they would react in a devastating situation until it happens to them.*

She tried to think of what she would say when she met him. Would her eyes automatically go to his leg? Would she run to his arms being worried that she'd knock him to the floor? Would she look into his eyes with pity? And just what would she say? *I've missed you so much Nick.* No—that's too generic. *Why didn't you call me—I've been frightened to death with worry.* No—using the word death is something he wished had happened anyhow. *Just be yourself, Jane. Walk up to him, take his face in your hands and gently kiss his lips. The rest will follow naturally.*

The next morning, Jane went to the airport and there was Marie standing by the curb with a glow on her face. "WOW, I guess you two had another honeymoon night."

"Why do you say that, Jane?"

"By the glow on your face. I'm so happy for you, Marie. He is one special man."

"Yes, he is; and you'll have your special man back in your life real soon."

"Let's get back to enjoying our trip. Fortunately, we have only 110 miles to our next stop. Let's just go back to our site and enjoy the afternoon. We can leave tomorrow morning for Barstow. There's not a lot to do in Barstow, which is good, as I'm presently very exhausted mentally and physically. There is a ghost town that we can visit. I guess it's a former 1880's silver-mining town."

"Whatever you want to do, Jane. I can't imagine what's going on in that cute head of yours right now. Let's just take it slow and easy. My target date for being back at the hacienda is August 8. I guess Vince has plans for my birthday the next day. Lord only knows what he'll cook up this year. Remember when he flew the four of us to Spain last year?"

"You bet I do. We had so much fun, but sometimes scary. How about that snake charmer in Tangier? I was so fascinated with the snake that the guy wanted me to learn how to charm it. I was so scared that I wanted to run, not be the snake's buddy."

"You did have a 'get me out of here' look. I also remember how you bargained for that rug that you didn't want. You were just playing with the merchant, but he outsmarted you and you had to buy it. There you were with a 6'X9' Persian rug and we had a plane to catch. Fortunately, you were able to bargain with another merchant, and sell it back for a lot more. You could do well at a business in Tangier."

"Sure. That's where I would want to live—NOT!"

Once they arrived back at their campsite, they spent the afternoon relaxing and reading their books. Vince called Marie letting her know that he had made it safely back to their hacienda. "How is Jane doing?"

"She seems to be okay. We're sitting out here on the patio enjoying the afternoon and reading our books. Fortunately, we have a short ride to our next stop. It's still in California. In fact, we have two more stops in Cali before heading to Arizona."

"I love how you ladies plan your stops. You always seem to take it easy which could imply that there would not be much in the area to tour. However, the stories that you tell me on your return from these adventures are intriguing."

"Jane does most of the planning and mapping. I just go along for the ride."

Jane was sitting next to Marie and was eavesdropping so shouted, "Hi, Vince. She's not telling you the truth, as I'd be lost without her navigating, her ideas, and suggestions. We're a great team."

Vince said to Marie that he was glad to hear the laughter in Jane's voice. "Now, all we have to do is get those two lovebirds back together again."

Marie had to watch her words with Jane sitting close by so just responded, "Ditto. We'll see you soon, honey." She then disconnected.

Jane looked at Marie and said, "You are truly a great friend, Marie. I know I couldn't have gotten through these past few weeks without your support and compassion. I don't think I've said it in a while but I'm so glad that you like this camping stuff. We've made some great memories over the years."

"Yes, we have. You sound like this will be our last one."

"I hope not, but we are living 2,000 miles apart now and we're not getting any younger. I just wanted you to know how special you are to me."

"And you to me. Now let's quit this mushy stuff and get back to our books. By the way, I'm getting hungry. Do we have anything to make our pu-pu platter?"

"I'll go inside and check. Are you ready for our afternoon cocktail?"

"I don't think you need to even ask. I'm always ready."

With that, Jane laughed and went inside.

When Jane came out with the snacks, she also had the directory. "I don't know why, but after our next stop in Needles, CA, I have us going over 300 miles. It takes us into Arizona. There's a campground 93 miles from Needles. Since there isn't much to do in Needles, would you mind if we just stay one night there? We wouldn't unhook and we can do the same in Blythe."

"I don't mind at all. How far is it from here to Needles?"

"140 miles. We go on I-40. Looking at the map, it appears to be a boring drive. Most of the way is through the Mojave Desert and only three tiny towns. They are so small that they aren't even listed in the map index."

"Maybe we should have the truck checked before we leave. It has been a while."

"That's an excellent idea, Marie. I saw a dealership close by. I'll call them now and see if we can get an appointment for early tomorrow."

Jane called, and they did have an opening. The next morning, the ladies headed for the dealership and explained that they would be on I-40 later that day. "Can you please make sure that the diesel fuel liquid has been removed, check the tires, the battery, etc?"

The mechanic supervisor looked at Jane as if to say, "I think I know how to do my job." He responded that his men would make sure the truck would be in mint condition.

The ladies saw a restaurant next door, so they decided to have breakfast while they waited. A while later, the mechanic called and said that the truck was ready for them. "We found everything to be in tip-top condition. You ladies have done a great job at keeping this beauty maintained. My men couldn't believe that two older women are touring the country in this masterpiece."

Jane responded, "This beauty pulls a 38' fifth wheel and does a fine job too."

"This truck could pull anything. We are all envious, ladies. Have a safe trip. Here is my card. Not that you will have any trouble, but if something happens within the first 75 miles, call us and we'll be there to fix it."

"I don't know if we should thank you for the offer or be scared."

"Trust me. You have nothing to worry about. Now go and enjoy yourselves."

The ladies stopped at a truck stop and filled their tank; and then went back to the campsite. As they were performing their departure chores, Jane said, "Marie, let's pack some sandwiches, chips, and water. We can eat in the truck as we're driving across the desert. That way, hopefully, we won't need to stop."

"I know that you told me, but how far is it again to our next stop?"

"140 miles. With the open road, we can go 60-70MPH. We'll be there in no time at all."

"Okay. Let's roll."

They hooked up and were on the road by 11:00.

Chapter Thirty

Everything went smoothly as they made their way to Needles and then on to Blythe.

That afternoon, they were enjoying the nice weather and reading their books while sitting out on the patio. Jane said, "This campground is really nice. That glass table top with wrought iron chairs over there will work really well for dinner; and I always love it when we can park our rig on a concrete pad. It's always a breeze to unhook when we pull in and hookup when we pull out."

"You always worry about that stuff, but we always manage to survive. Changing the subject, just look at the flowing Colorado River."

"I remember when I went backpacking on the North Rim of Grand Canyon. We were at 7,000' elevation and made our way down to the Colorado. When we started setting up camp, the guide told us we had better go up hill another 50' from the river. We asked why, and he explained that a dam had been installed many miles away, forcing the river sometimes to rise 20' to 25' in one day. Fortunately, we did that; and, the next morning the river was only about 30' below us. We looked at the river, and many of us just shivered at what could have happened."

"I remember you telling me about that. You could have been swept away in the Colorado. That would not have been a good thing to have happen."

"We had a few close calls along the five-day trip, but it was an experience of a lifetime. I was 40 years old at the time and only agreed to go, after I found out that a medical doctor and Cardiologist were going to be in our group."

"That's Jane. Always making sure that she's covered all of the bases."

"I hope you don't get upset, but I changed our itinerary again."

"What did you do now?"

"Since we decided to come here to Blythe, that takes us on our way to Phoenix instead of Flagstaff. While we've been to both places in the past, we haven't been to Tucson. I also figured that you could visit with your brother and niece again while we're in Phoenix. We would be arriving there Thursday, July 27. We could do our standard Monday/Thursday routine and leave July 31, or whenever you wish. If we do leave 7/31, we would head for Benson, Arizona. Have you and Vince been to Benson?"

"No, we haven't. In fact, we haven't really toured the surrounding states. Vince travels so much that when he's home, we like to just chill and enjoy each other."

"I can thoroughly understand that one. There's lots to see in and around Benson, like the O.K. Corral, Kartchner Caverns and an old copper mine near the Mexican border. We could spend a week in Benson and just stay overnight in Las Cruces, New Mexico. If you remember, about all there is to see would be the missile range and White Sands National Monument. While they're both great to see, we've already been there and done that. If we do this itinerary, we would have you back at your hacienda August 8."

"Thank you for restructuring everything to get me home by August 9; but do we need to be specific? I've always liked how we enjoy some areas so we stay longer. If we don't like where we are, we just pack up and leave. That's been the wonderful luxury of owning this rig."

"That's fine. I just want to make sure that you are home by August 9 or Vince will be very upset with me. Changing the subject, look at that beautiful sun starting to set. I've always enjoyed the western sunsets. They're so colorful with the clouds in different formations. They make bluish and pinkish hues."

"Then, there are sometimes orange and yellow hues," commented Marie.

"I'm getting hungry, Marie. How about I get out the grill that's a nightmare to hook up, and we roast some chicken?"

"That sounds good. I'll go inside and prepare our potatoes with green onion and garlic."

The ladies enjoyed their nice dinner sitting out on the patio. Afterward Marie asked, "Do we have any leftover firewood?"

"I do think there's a few pieces. I'll go check."

While Jane was checking for firewood, Marie took the dishes into the rig and cleaned up the kitchen.

Jane started the fire in the fire ring, then tackled taking down the grill. As they were sitting around the warm fire, Jane commented, "That grill is going to get the best of me yet. I'm half tempted to buy one of those small charcoal grills and forget wrestling with that damn RV grill of ours."

"Whatever floats your boat, Jane. However, the disadvantage of that approach, is always buying charcoal and lighter plus having to store it—in addition to the grill that we already have—I might add. Presently, we use the campground's propane, so no extra cost."

"Well, you crawl under the rig the next time and try to connect the hose from the rig to the grill. It's no picnic."

"Let's just call it a night. I'm anxious to get on the road again. I'm only a few days away from seeing my sweetheart. Speaking of sweetheart, I assume you haven't heard from Nick's friends in Italy or you would have said something."

"I was thinking of calling the Frenchman. I believe he said his name was Jean Claude. Nick always teases me when he's at his chalet, that he's nine hours ahead of me. With my A-type personality, I always seem to be moving fast, so he loves to say that he's faster than me. Thinking of the time difference, I guess I had better wait until tomorrow. By the way, I think Jean Claude lives in France. Melina sounds Swiss, but it sounded like she lives with Jean Claude. In the past two months, it appears as if Nick has a whole new life and set of friends. I need to get back with him soon or I may lose him forever. Life surely has its twists and turns. After all those years, Nick and I finally agree to marry and then the rug is pulled out from underneath us. It's not fair."

"I believe I've said it many times, but there are times through life when we hit a snag. The secret is to bounce back and learn from it."

"Right now, I don't see where this situation will teach me anything."

"Let's call it a night, Jane. Put out the fire and let's crash."

Chapter Thirty One

Wwhile the ladies were traveling, Vince was planning Marie's birthday party. He knew how much she loved going up in the hot air balloon and had given her many lessons. Marie had made friends with the owner of the gift shop at the museum. Her name was Florence. She had come up with the idea of having a festival in Marie's honor. Vince went into the gift shop to see how the event plans were coming along. Florence was waiting on a customer so he signaled to her. She found another clerk to help the customer and went over to Vince. "Good to see you, Vince. I suppose you would like an update on the party."

"That would be nice. Marie and her friend, Jane, are scheduled to arrive August 8. After my discussion with you about dates, we agreed on August 10. You volunteered to coordinate how many hot air balloonists would be attending."

"I did do that, didn't I. Well, I couldn't believe how everyone stepped up to the plate. So far, we have 92 of them with 12 more possibilities."

"Marie will be so surprised when she sees them all floating just for her. Since she moved here, she has been so involved with the museum. My buying her very own hot air balloon will be such a surprise. So, what festivities have you planned?"

"I thought we'd have a lobster and steak grill fest out behind the museum. Of course, we'd have to do this after closing. That's why, doing it during the week will work better for everyone."

"It sounds like you have everything going smoothly. Don't hesitate to let me know if you need anything. I'll be out of town all next week, but scheduled to be home the week of the party. In the interim, you can call me anytime."

"Don't worry. I will."

"Thanks again for all you do and have done. It's much appreciated. Remember to spare no expense. Nothing is too good for my sweetheart."

Vince went to his hacienda and let his staff know about the party plans; and when Marie was expected home. He decided to call Franceau and see how Nick was doing. "As you know, I'm Nick's best friend in the states. I'm giving a birthday party for my wife, Marie, on August 10. Is there any way that Nick would be able to attend the party?"

"Nick has been making fantastic progress. In fact, he's been walking daily without supervision. He has a very steady balance and regaining his positive attitude, but has a long way to go. If the party were held here, there'd be no problem. However, it's the plane ride that I'm sure would give him grief. You wouldn't believe how much he shook and sweated when he came home from Paris and that flight was only two hours."

"Yes, but wasn't that the same flight path that he took when the plane crashed?"

"No. He was going from Switzerland to Paris."

"Ohh, yes. Now I remember. We are just getting anxious to get him and Jane back together again. I thought the party would be a great way to do that. I have a staff to help him. In fact, it would be wonderful if you would come with him. I know, it's a pipe dream but am praying that it can become a reality."

"What date did you say?"

"August 10. Can I talk to Nick?"

"He's out walking. Let me talk to him when he comes back. I'll tell him that you called, but not the reason why. Don't mention anything about the party or your wanting him there. Just say you're calling to chat because you miss the old times."

While Franceau and Vince were talking, Nick walked into the room. He stood there listening and then asked, "Is that Vince on the phone?"

"Yes, it is. He's concerned about you, Nick."

"Let me have the phone."

Franceau handed the phone to Nick and he said, "Leave me alone, Vince. I no longer have a life in the states so quit calling me."

"I'm so sorry that you were in a plane crash; and that you feel your former life is gone. If there was a way that I could turn back time to obliterate that tragedy, I would. You are a special friend and no matter what you say, you'll always be my best friend. We had so many fun times, Nick. Remember that trip last year to Spain? Jane's scared to death of snakes and yet she was fascinated by the snake charmer. She about jumped on your back when he suggested teaching her how to do it."

"Quit hashing over old times. That's exactly what they are. Forget everything we ever did together."

"I can't do that and I know for a fact that you can't either. Please come back to the states, Nick. We're family and miss you terribly. I'm throwing a big party August 10 for Marie's birthday. Her best present would be to see you."

"I don't want to see any of you and will never go to the states again. Don't call me or contact me anymore, Vince. Our friendship is dead. Goodbye."

Nick disconnected the call and went storming to his bedroom. He slammed the bedroom door and brooded for many hours. Franceau, Jean Claude and Melina tried to get him to come down to the study, but he wouldn't even answer the door or respond. Even Gabritta tried to bribe him with food, but to no avail.

That evening Franceau just entered without knocking. Nick was sitting by the window just staring out at the sky. Franceau pulled up a chair and didn't say a word. After a while Nick said, "Isn't that a beautiful sky?"

"Yes, it is."

"Why wouldn't I have had that beautiful sky last June 5? Maybe I would still have two legs and my wonderful sweetheart, Jane."

"No one can predict what will happen tomorrow. We have to accept what will be and move on. Almost always, it ends up being much better."

"How can you say that this thing attached to my leg is better for me?"

"Would you have known Jean Claude and Melina, had this not happened; and what about me? I love my new position and am pretty sure you love having me take care of all of these many businesses that you have been juggling for many years."

"You have been a Godsend, Franceau. I have to admit that you've increased the profitability with most of them. The remaining ones, I just have as a write-off."

"There, see? Now think of that sweetheart of yours. You know that she loves you inside and out. Just think about how she's feeling right now. I'm sure she'd be upset and hurt terribly with your thinking she wouldn't want you as you are now. Jean Claude talked to her and she is wrought with worry."

"Why would Jean Claude talk to her; and how did he even know how to get her cell number?"

"It all originated when you called Vince about that trust fund. All of us want you and Jane back together again. Your present state is affecting all of us and we want to get back to our lives."

"Okay. Just let me do some meditating. I know I've been a cantankerous fool. I'm sure Gabritta has prepared some special dinner for our guests. Feeling sorry for myself all day has made me hungry. I'll be down in a little while. Please apologize to Jean Claude and Melina for my deserting them. I invite them here for a few days and then ignore them."

"Yes, you've been rude, but we all have been living with your moods. We look forward to the renewed Nicholas Camboli. That Nicholas Cambini was not a very nice man." Franceau left the room and closed the door."

God, what should I do? I miss that beautiful Jane so much, but I'm so afraid she'll be ashamed of me or embarrassed to be around a cripple. It was then that Nick felt a small breeze and he had a chill run down his spine. It was as if something said, "It is okay. You two were meant for each other. You just need to go to her; and don't worry about the flight as I'll take care of you."

Nick went down to the dining room and sat at the head of the table. Franceau entered the room and looked at Nick. "What happened to you?"

"What do you mean?"

"You just have a look as if a huge burden has been lifted from your shoulders."

"I think it has. Let's have dinner and I'll tell you what just happened."

Jean Claude and Melina then entered the room and sat down. Melina said, "Nick, you must be feeling better."

"Yes, I am, Melina. I just had a talk with God up in my bedroom. I promise, things will be different from now on. In fact, I just might take Vince up on that offer to attend Marie's birthday party August 10."

They all chimed in, "WOW, a miracle has just happened. Melina started to tear up and then everyone clapped."

Nick called in Gabritta and told her to go down to the wine cellar and get those bottles of wine that he had been saving. When she returned with them, everyone celebrated Nick's coming back to the living.

While they were having dessert, Nick went to his study and called Vince.

"To begin with, I want to apologize for the way that I've been treating you."

"There's no need to apologize, Nick. Who knows how I would have reacted had I been in your shoes."

"I wasn't in a good state of mind these past few weeks. I guess you could say that I had an ahh-hah moment today. I finally realized that I needed to snap out of it; and go on with my life, or retreat into a shell and exist with no friends or family. I chose the former. You've been a great friend, Vince, and I don't want to lose that friendship. I especially don't want to lose the only love and soul mate that I had."

"Those ahh-hah moments sometimes take a while to surface; and I'm just glad that you had yours."

"I would love to come to the states, but there are two huge factors to overcome."

"And what are those?"

"I had a terrible time getting on the plane from Paris to my chateau. I don't know if I can bring myself to be on a plane for 15 hours."

"Would you feel more comfortable if I had my pilot fly over to get you?"

"Let me get this straight. You would have your pilot fly your plane for 15 hours just to get me and then fly for another 15 hours back to Albuquerque? This isn't just a hop, skip, and a jump, Vince."

"I understand that, but would be willing to do it just to get you here. I would ask one favor though. That you allow my pilot to stay at your chateau one or two days so he could get his bearings to fly you back."

"If I did agree to such an absurd arrangement, and you do know that I'm kidding; there would be one more hurdle to overcome."

"And what is that?"

"I'm petrified at how Jane would react to my altered body."

"How many years have you known Jane? Has she ever mocked those with disabilities? NO. In fact, over the years, she has helped many overcome their fears and regain confidence in themselves. She would be your best medicine. I believe we've all been saying that to you for weeks. You just wouldn't listen."

"I'm still scared, Vince."

"And I'm sure that Jane's scared you'll read something negative in her eyes that isn't there. Just be calm. Don't be defensive. Things will work out. Now, when do you want me to send over that plane?"

"You said that the party is, August 10. Right?"

"Yes, that's right."

"I need to talk to Franceau to make sure I'm not doing something that will harm my progress. By the way, can he come with me?"

"Of course he can."

"Don't mention to Marie or Jane that I am considering this endeavor. It's a huge step for me and I'm still not sure that I can do it."

"Attitude is so important, Nick. You just need that confidence and say, yes I can."

"Thanks again, Vince, for being such an understanding friend. I'll get back to you."

"After Nick canceled the cell phone call, he went back to the dining room and told everyone the conversation that he just had with Vince.

Jean Claude said, "While it's wonderful that you had this ahh-hah moment, I wonder if you're moving too fast."

Melina said, "Nick, I know you're a very strong and determined individual. You proved that after the plane crash. We all could possibly be dead had you not done the things that you did."

Nick responded, "Why do I feel that there's a but coming."

"Ever since entering the hospital in Paris, you didn't want to live and wouldn't do anything the doctors and nurses told you to do. You threw things. You were a terrible patient and the nurses couldn't wait until you left. Even after coming back here, you gave Franceau and Gabritta grief. Now you want to flip a switch and be your old self. I'm concerned that tomorrow, you'll be back to that nasty self."

Nick asked Franceau, "You've been pretty quiet throughout this conversation. You're the expert. What do you think?"

"I think it's the best medicine for you. You need your friends in the states more than ever right now. If Vince is willing to have his pilot fly you there, what more could a friend ask. Those private planes are nothing like the commercial ones. They are safer and no question about the comfort. Good for you, Nick. I am so proud that I could burst."

"That's not necessary, Franceau, but thanks for your opinion. Would you go with me to the states?"

"It would be my honor. When would we be leaving?"

"Vince is throwing a huge birthday party for Marie August 10. I would like to attend. If the pilot flew here August 6, he would need to rest at least one day. The flight is about 15 hours so we'd be cutting it close if we left August 8. Let me talk to Vince and see what he says."

"Sounds good to me," said Franceau. Jean Claude and Melina were happy for Nick and glad that Franceau found it to be good medicine.

Nick asked Jean Claude and Melina if they would also like to go on this journey. Jean Claude whispered to Melina and she shook her head, no. "Thanks for the offer, Nick, but we really need to get back to our jobs in France. You've been a gracious host during our stay at this awesome chateau but we need to get back to reality."

Nick called Vince back. "My physical therapist says being with all of you would be the best medicine for me."

"This is wonderful news. I'll coordinate everything and let you know what's going on."

Chapter Thirty Two

The ladies made it to Phoenix in good time, but hit a snag as they were going through the town. They were on I-10 and were supposed to pick up Route 60. Somehow they got on Route 202 and followed that route for over an hour. That finally brought them back on I-10. However, they were south of Phoenix and they were supposed to be east to find Apache Junction. Marie apologized for getting them lost.

"You didn't get us lost, Marie. For some reason, the GPS wanted us to stay on I-10. This is the first time it has led us astray. Let's get off at the next exit and turn around. It's only noon, so we have plenty of time to find the campground."

Marie looked at the city map and said, "Head north on I-10 and then take a right onto I-202 bypass. After a few miles, you'll see Route 60. Take a right and it takes us to the campground. Sometimes using the old fashioned way works the best."

Once they made it to the entrance of the campground, Jane said, "Good job, Marie. Another blip has been corrected. I remember this place now. We stayed here a couple of years ago. No concrete pads, but they do a nice job of leveling the gravel sites."

The ladies checked in at the small office and were given their site number. Once parked, Marie got out of the truck and put blocks under the wheels of the RV. She then went back to the bed of the truck, pulled on the handle of the hitch and it disconnected. She removed the safety chain and unplugged the electric cord. "You can pull ahead now, Jane. It's my turn to say, good job."

They proceeded to do their arrival chores. Once they were inside, Jane pushed the buttons for the slides to move out. "We really do have a nice little home, don't we Marie?"

"We sure do. After all of the research we did before buying this one, we ended up with perfection. What's your most favorite thing in this rig?"

"I guess I would have to say, the breakfast bar and all of the counter space in the kitchen. It's so easy to prepare food in it and we can even have two of us doing it at the same time. What's your favorite?"

"That large shower with skylight, of course. There's so much room to move around in. Thinking of something else, I'll call my brother and see if he would have time for me tomorrow. Do you want to go with me?"

"Why don't you stay overnight with his family. They could bring you back Saturday afternoon and we could have a barbeque outside using that fabulous grill of ours. While you're gone, I'll go and buy all of the goodies."

"Why do you want me to leave. Are you trying to get rid of me, Jane?"

"Yes, I am. I love you dearly but I need some time alone. I want my Nick and I need to understand what has happened and how to fix it."

"That makes sense. For now, let's just relax for the rest of the day." As they were sitting outside in their chairs, Marie called her brother. He was excited to hear from her and said he would come over the next day and get her.

The weekend went smoothly. Marie enjoyed seeing her brother, nieces and nephews. They all came to the rig on Saturday and had an enjoyable time visiting together.

The ladies prepared for leaving the following Monday. Since they had already been on Route 202 to I-10, it was a breeze going on their way to Benson, Arizona.

While traveling, Jane asked Marie, "As we're getting closer and closer to your home, are you getting excited?"

"I sure am; and I wonder what my sweetheart has up his sleeve to make my birthday this year even grander than last year. I hope it's not traveling, as I've had enough of that for a while. I don't know about you, but the older I get, the harder this is getting. We do try to relax, but I think we really need to do more of it on our trips."

"You're probably right, Marie. Remember when we first started camping 25 years ago? I'd call you on a spur of the moment, and we'd pack our limited stuff in the car. Then the tent would be set up and everything in place within minutes. We even slept on the floor."

"Yes, I do remember. Then, as the years went by, we'd have more and more stuff. We even advanced to having cots and a porta-potty; and don't forget the outside shower house that we bought."

"I did forget about that. We did have a lot of stuff, didn't we?"

"Yes, we did. When we did a test run of renting a motor home, we were set up in 20 minutes. We were both shocked; but trying to put up that manual awning was a joke. It slammed against the rig and about scared us half to death. People from neighboring sites came running to see what happened."

"That was embarrassing, but we did get to meet all of them and hear their stories of screw ups. We sure have had some fun times over the years."

"You make it sound like this is our last trip, Jane."

"I don't mean to, but we're no spring chickens anymore. I'm sure we'll have many more trips. I'll just make sure that Nick stays home or goes with us every time. Would you mind if he went with us, Marie?"

"Of course not. We could even have Vince join us, if he wanted to."

"Here we are, not even back to your place yet and we're talking about our next trip. Not meaning to change the subject, but aren't we getting closer to our next campground? I haven't seen the typical camping sign along the highway. Did you happen to see it?"

"Yes, I did. The book says it's easy access off I-10." Just then another sign popped up telling them to exit. They drove a little ways down the road and found their next campground. They performed their arrival duties and then were again in their chairs relaxing.

"I believe I told you what all we can see while we're here. Right, Marie?"

"Yes. Already you have us going, going, going."

"Sorry about that. By the way, I haven't asked you lately, about how that foot of yours is doing."

"It's fine. Surprisingly, it hasn't bothered me much at all; but then we've been in semi-arid climates. That has a lot to do with how good or bad it feels."

"Then it was a good idea for you to move from soggy Ohio to semi-arid New Mexico."

"Now that you mentioned it, I have felt pretty good since moving to the hacienda. It very seldom rains there. In fact, I do miss the rain once in a while."

The ladies did their touring thing the next two days and then were on their way to Las Cruces, New Mexico.

As they were traveling, Marie asked, "Would you mind if we didn't unhook this afternoon? I want to get home. We could be on the road tomorrow by 8:00AM and be at the hacienda by 2:00-3:00."

"Of course I mind—just kidding! Besides, I'm anxious to see what Vince has up his sleeve relating to your birthday."

Chapter Thirty Three

The ladies did make it safely to the hacienda. As they were driving up into the hills, Jane said, "I forgot how beautiful it is up here. You are one lucky gal, Marie."

"Yes, I am." They pulled up to the front of the hacienda; and there was Vince waiting patiently. He ran out to the truck, opened the door and practically pulled Marie out of the cab. He planted a big kiss on her lips, pulled away and then said, "I'm so glad that you're home. He was walking her inside and it dawned on him about greeting Jane. "I'm so rude, Jane, come on in."

"That's quite okay, Vince. I would react the same if my Nick was standing here. Where would you like me to park this big rig?"

"You can just leave it there. I'll have one of my hired hands park it for you."

Once they were inside and Vince fixed them a drink. He said, "Your mentioning Nick is a good segway for what I'm about to say."

Jane said, "The start of this conversation brings back not-so-good memories. I hope you can do better the second time around."

"I'm sure I can. Right now, as we speak, your Nick is on my plane heading here. It's a 15 hour flight so he should be arriving sometime tomorrow morning. He is scared to death about flying and is worried at how you'll react to his altered body. That's the only reason why he never wanted to come back."

"What changed his mind?"

"He said that he had an ahh-hah moment and decided to live again. He can tell you all about it when he arrives."

Jane downed her drink and asked for another one. "I think this will be the longest night of my life."

"Don't worry, Jane. We can stay up all night, if you want."

"Let's unpack the rig first before it gets moved. You can show me where I should put all of my stuff; and then let's decide what to do next."

While Marie was taking a shower the next morning, Vince told Jane about the surprise party he was throwing for Marie the next evening. She asked, "Is there anything I can do to help with the festivities?"

"Thanks, but I think we've got it covered. Marie's friend at the museum has coordinated the entire event. One of my guys helped me find a hot air balloon for Jane."

"YOU'VE GOT TO BE KIDDING. REALLY??—WOW!"

"Do you think it's too much?"

"Hell, no. Marie loves those things. She'll be so excited."

Just then, Marie walked into the room. "What's going on? You two look like you swallowed a canary."

179

Vince said, "Nothing's going on. We were just chatting."

Jane said to Vince, "I wonder where your plane is with Nick right now."

"My pilot radioed that the flight was going smoothly and Nick had slept most of the way. They are now over North Carolina and should be here by early afternoon."

"I hope you two don't mind, but I need to go for a walk."

Marie said, "You do whatever makes you feel comfortable. We'll just be here catching up on each other's lives."

Jane walked outside and admired the beautiful blue sky. There were some hot air balloonists flying high. Their colors were so bright and beautiful. She looked around at the foothills and decided to head down towards the museum. When she entered the gift shop, she asked for the owner. "I am the owner," said Florence. Jane said, "I'm Marie's traveling companion."

"It's great to meet you. Marie has told me so much about you and all of the many adventures that you two have had over the years."

"We really have been blessed with many opportunities."

Vince tells me that you've done an outstanding job of coordinating Marie's birthday party. Are there any last minute things that I can do to help?"

"Thank you for offering, but I believe we have everything in place. It is really going to be quite a birthday party. I guess you could even call it Marie's own balloon festival. She has learned how to navigate one of those things and Vince has bought one of her very own."

"Yes, he told me. Marie has never mentioned to me that she had lessons. That's really strange as I thought we shared everything."

"Maybe she didn't want you to feel bad that she could do something awesome without you."

"Well, I had better get back up to the hacienda. My sweetheart is flying in from Italy as we speak; and I want to be there when he gets off the plane."

Jane then hiked back up to the hacienda in time to see the plane landing on Vince's private landing strip. She ran out to the plane and stood at the bottom of the steps. She couldn't believe her eyes when Nick started coming down. She started crying and ran up to meet him. She almost knocked him over and started kissing him, first on the cheek, then the neck. She worked her way down and even kissed his artificial lower leg.

"Take it easy, Jane. I want to have a chance to kiss you."

"I'm sorry, Nick; but you have no idea how much I've missed you. I was so afraid that I had lost you."

"Let's get off these stairs so I can hug you."

Once they were on the ground, they kissed and embraced for the longest time. Nick pulled away, looked lovingly into her eyes and said, "You have been constantly on my mind these past weeks."

She put her arms around him, squeezed him and said, "Then why didn't you call me? I was frantic with worry." She was looking at Franceau, as he was coming down the stairs, as if to say, *who are you?*

Fortunately, Nick saw her expression, so he ignored the question and said, "Jane meet Franceau. He was my physical therapist in the hospital. Now that he managed to get me walking again, I've hired him to become my assistant in Italy."

"Glad to meet you, Franceau."

She looked at Nick and asked him what had happened to James."

"He's still at my home in Florida. I was getting too many businesses for James to juggle, so I separated the ones from America. James handles those and Franceau deals with the rest of them."

Franceau said, "Glad to meet you, Jane. You don't know how much all of us have looked forward to seeing you two together again. Nick was a long-lost soul for many weeks and made everyone's lives miserable. It's so wonderful to see the glow on his face. We knew that you would be his best medicine."

"Have you been a bad boy, Nick?"

He ignored the question and said, "Look, there's a car coming for us."

"I see how you keep changing the subject when I ask a question."

"I didn't notice that I was doing that."

Jane said, "Yeah, right, then kissed him again."

Just then, the car pulled up alongside them. One of Vince's hired hands opened the door for them all to get in and drove them back to the hacienda.

Vince and Marie were so excited to see Jane and Nick stuck like glue to each other. Marie said, "I guess we should get used to their being one for a while. Let's go inside." Once they all sat down, Marie continued,

"This is so exciting. You are my best birthday present ever, Nick."

Vince said, "I guess that puts me in second place. At this moment I couldn't think of a better place to be."

Nick said, "You guys are all too kind. There was a time, not long ago, when I wished I was dead. I'm so glad there were people like Franceau to force me to live." He looked at Jane while he said, "Having this beauty by my side is like a dream come true." Nick bent down and kissed Jane on the lips. She snuggled closer to him and said, "I never want to leave your side again."

After dinner, they all went out to the veranda and enjoyed the beautiful outdoor fireplace. Marie looked at Vince with a gleam in here eyes, snuggled up against him and asked, "So what's in store for me tomorrow? Are we jet setting someplace?"

"Actually, we're just staying home tomorrow. I think Nick has had enough jet setting for a few days; plus you and Jane probably want to stay stationary for a while."

"I find that hard to believe. No fireworks, no 15-piece orchestra, no people?"

"How did you know? I wanted to keep it a surprise."

"Are you really doing all of that?"

Jane responded, "All of that and more. You won't believe it, Marie. I think he did outdo your last year's party and then some."

Marie had the biggest grin on her face and said, "Let's all go to bed. I'm anxious to get to sleep so tomorrow will come quicker."

Everyone went down to the museum the next day at 10:00. When they arrived, they saw over 90 balloons setting up in a huge field. Marie asked Vince if his men had theirs set up. "Actually, Marie, let's walk over to where they are. I want to show you something. Nick, Jane and Franceau followed them over to a very colorful balloon. It had Marie's name in huge letters. "I don't believe my eyes," was her reply. "I have my very own balloon?"

"Yes you do, sweetheart. It's a perfect day for going up. Are you ready to join the others?"

"You bet I am. Can Nick, Jane, and Franceau join us?"

"If they want to."

Franceau was eager to do it as he had never been in a hot air balloon. In fact, he had never even seen one. Nick and Jane decided to stay on the ground and just watch the festivities.

As all of the balloons started to climb, Jane took lots of pictures; and waved to Marie as she ascended into the air. Marie was singing and waving to everyone.

Jane said to Nick, "That's the most expression I've seen Marie make in years. I guess Vince really did outdo himself."

"By the looks of all of the grills and bar being set up, I think the festivities are just getting started."

When Marie and Vince each landed their balloons, they saw lots of guests partaking in the food and enjoying the band. There were even couples dancing on a makeshift dance floor out under a tree of lights. They walked over to the happy couple, and Marie said, "It looks like the party is going to go well into the night. It could even become a wedding for the happy couple."

Jane said, "While that's a great idea, Marie, I think Nick's family would be upset if they missed Nick's wedding. Remember, he's never been married and the family would want to be involved with the big event. Do you agree, Nick?"

"I want to marry you as quickly as possible before something else comes between us; but yes, they would really be angry at both of us."

The chefs were famous and Vince had them come from all around the world. The food was prepared exquisitely and everyone partied well into the night.

Jane could tell that Nick was getting tired, so she asked Vince if one of his men could drive them back to the hacienda. "Of course," was the reply. Jane and Nick hugged Marie and wished her a happy birthday.

As they were driving away, Franceau walked up to Vince and said, "I can't believe the change in Nick. All of us were concerned that maybe this trip was too soon but he is just glowing. It was the best medicine ever. Thank you, Vince. You are truly a great friend."

"I'm just so happy that he turned himself around to be the old Nick again. I really missed that fella."

"Let's cut out the mushy stuff and quit putting a damper on my party," was Marie's comment. "I'm still in disbelief that I have my very own hot air balloon. I never thought it would be possible. You are always amazing me, Vince, with your kindness and creativity. This party is awesome!"

"You have Florence to thank for all of it. I just paid for it."

Many of the guests had torn down their balloons and left the party. It was well after midnight when they all headed back to the hacienda. Marie said, "I wonder if Jane and Nick are planning their wedding."

The guys chimed in, "They're probably doing more than that."

"I am sure that they are," was her reply.

When they arrived back at the hacienda, they made lots of noise to let the lovebirds know they had returned. Nick and Jane came down the stairs hand in hand. "Welcome back everyone. Did you have fun, Marie?"

"Fun doesn't even start to explain the thrills that I had. This day will definitely be remembered as one of the best birthdays I ever had."

"So, it's not the best one?" asked Vince.

"Well, my sweetheart, I want you to keep trying to outdo the year before."

"Just like a woman, always wanting more."

Jane and Marie chimed in, "Yep, that's us."

Franceau pulled Nick over to the side of the room and asked if it would be possible for him to go to Florida and work with James. "I've completed my physical therapy duties; and it looks like Jane has taken over. You've done remarkably well with the flight and dealing with change. I need to get back to my other duties that you assigned to me. I thought, if I met with James for a few days, we could wrap up some loose ends."

"Do you want me to go with you?"

"No. You stay here and enjoy your sweetheart and friends. I'll keep you apprised of the latest deals. You just rest and relax. You've been through so much that I don't want to see any setbacks."

"Nor do I."

Jane walked over to see what they were discussing. "Is everything okay?"

Nick said, "Franceau was just telling me how he was going to go meet James in Florida and wrap up some business deals we've been doing. Everything's fine, honey. Let's call it a day as I'm exhausted."

Over the next few days, Marie helped Jane plan her wedding. Jane said, "Nick and I decided on a September date. It'll be at his chateau in Italy under a huge tent at the rear of his property. Overlooking Lake Como will be breathtaking. The weather can be brisk at that time of year, but we don't want to wait any longer. Nick said that the tent can be heated and he saw no problem with the date. I thought I would wear a cream colored suit with long skirt and flowers in my hair.

I need to tell you something, Marie. I can't imagine what Nick's been through these past weeks; and I understand that his mental state has been on shaky grounds. However, I can't, in good conscience, marry him without telling him about Frank."

"But, you told me that there was nothing to tell."

"There isn't, but what if Frank called or showed up one day, what would I say?"

"To begin with, I think it's unlikely that he would show up in Ohio or Italy, for that matter; and, if he calls, you can cut the conversation short. DON'T TELL NICK, at least not now. If it still bothers you a year from now, then do it, BUT NOT NOW. Okay??"

"I don't agree with you; but I'll keep still about it, for now."

"THANK YOU!"

"Now, let's get back to the subject at hand. Of course you're invited to the wedding. In fact, you're going to be my matron of honor. Is that okay?"

"I would be honored to be your matron of honor. Any more honors?"

"Cute!"

"Regarding the reception, Nick was impressed with the chefs at your birthday party so he'll ask Vince for their names and contact information."

"I believe the guys are taking care of the reception details. Vince said he already had a dress rehearsal with my party; and Nick told him that he wanted to help you. I guess the staff in Italy used to coordinate all the parties that Nick would have for his business acquaintances. He said that they have a system down to a science and not to worry."

"Famous last words. You know how I like to be in control of things, but I'll restrain myself. Let's go to a stationary store and select the wedding invitations."

"I have just the right place. A friend out here threw a big party and I helped. She used a place that was fabulous. Since I don't drive anymore, Vince has arranged to have one of his men chauffeur me whenever and wherever I want to go."

"Well, ain't that special!"

Chapter Thirty Four

The ladies mailed 100 wedding invitations; and had done all the planning that they could from the states. The four of them were sitting around the breakfast table, and Jane asked Nick if he was up for another flight. "If I can fly in Vince's private jet and have my happy pills, I'll be fine. Are you ready to move to my chateau in Italy?"

"I hadn't really planned that far in advance. I've been concentrating on the wedding plans and didn't think about what happens afterwards."

"Well, it's a 15 hour flight in a private jet; and I'm sure it's much longer to go commercial, so I think you really need to start thinking of what to do. It's not a hop, skip, and jump."

"Let's let Marie and Vince have some space. I need to go shower and get dressed. Would you like to accompany me to our guest room?"

"Now, that's an offer I can't refuse."

Once they entered the bedroom, Jane asked Nick to sit on the bed. He started to shake, as if he was going to get some bad news. Jane had decided to tell him about Frank, anyhow; but seeing his expression, she changed her mind.

"Is there something you want to tell me, Jane?"

"I'm just wondering if we're moving too fast with this wedding. NO, I'm NOT BACKING OUT, so don't worry. I haven't been back at my home in Ohio for over two months; and the way things are going, it's going to be another 2-3 months. With your asking me about moving to Italy, sort of scares me. I would never want to lose my US citizenship."

"Well, if that's your only concern, I have that solved. You see, I have a dual citizenship and can arrange the same for you."

"You always know how to simplify things. I love you so very very much, Nick Camboli, or whatever your name is. By the way, what name would I be taking?"

"I'm glad that you don't want to keep your last name. I'll have James handle the legal aspects of changing my last name back to Camboli. Would that make you feel better?"

"Yes, it would. You always know how to take care of me, Nicholas Camboli. Now, let's make use of this bed."

"That's an offer that I can't refuse."

Chapter Thirty Five

Franceau and James wrapped up what outstanding deals they had, and then flew out to Albuquerque to meet up with Nick and Jane. They were so pleased to see Nick's continued improvement.

Vince told the guys of the upcoming plans to fly back to Nick's chateau in Italy. "We'll let you rest one or two days; but we really need to get to Italy. Jane's getting nervous about how the wedding plans are going. Gabritta informed her that the huge tent had been ordered and the mechanical experts were scheduled to set up heating and lighting the week before the wedding. She told Jane that the climate could be brisk, but she felt that the guests would be plenty warm. After all, when over 100 people will be congregating, it will be plenty warm."

Jane and Marie had gone to the bridal salon after Marie's birthday and were fitted for their suits. They were told that the suits would be finished by the end of August. "You'll have them in plenty of time before you leave to go to Italy. We guarantee that they will fit beautifully, on one condition. Neither of you can gain or lose any weight." The ladies just laughed at that comment and said, "There are no guarantees from our side." Everyone laughed at their response.

Jane and Marie had visited a florist in town so they could select the flower arrangements that Jane had in mind. Once that was accomplished, she had the florist email the selections to the florist that Nick had recommended in Italy. She was curious as to why he had a favorite florist. "I've had many needs for flowers over the years," was his response. She teased him over that comment.

The bridal salon called the end of August to schedule the ladies' fittings. Marie cried when Jane came out of the fitting room. "Do I look that bad, Marie?"

"Oh, no, Jane. Nick won't believe his eyes when he sees you. That cream colored suit is perfect. Let's get back to the hacienda as we have a plane to catch."

Jane thanked the salon owner for the excellent job and they were on their way.

Vince's pilot informed him that the plane was ready for boarding. There was Vince, Marie, Nick, Jane, Franceau and James. One of Vince's maids volunteered to go along and be their flight attendant. The weather was perfect and they encountered very little turbulence all the way to Italy.

Once they arrived, Nick was pleased to see Jean Claude and Melina. "I'm so excited to see you two. Jane, I want you to meet Jean Claude and Melina."

Jane went up to each of them and hugged them tightly. "I've heard so much about you. Melina, you hold a special place in Nick's heart, even though he gave you grief while at the hospital and even afterwards."

"Yes, he was a bear for a long time; but I'm so glad to see how happy and content he is now. You are his life, Jane. He was miserable without you."

Jean Claude said, "And what about me? Did Nick not mention my name at all?"

"Of course he did. He especially talked about your venture down the mountain; or at least trying to get down the mountain."

Nick heard the conversation, looked at his friend and said, "There's no way that I could ever forget you, old buddy. Let's go meet with the rest of the guests that had arrived. Jane said, "You socialize with them, sweetheart, while Marie and I go find Gabritta. I'm anxious to see how the wedding plans are going." Melina asked if she could join them. "Of course," was the answer.

They found Gabritta in the kitchen. She was talking to some of the caterers about how Nick wanted the food to be prepared and served. Jane introduced Marie and Melina to Gabritta. "How about we all walk out to the tent. I'm anxious to see it." Gabritta took them outside to one of the golf carts and they rode out to the huge tent at the rear of the property. Jane started to tear up as she couldn't believe how beautiful everything was. "You've done a spectacular job, Gabritta. It looks like you've covered every detail. "There were many people involved with this historical event. Nick's Italian family had a huge hand in its preparation."

As they entered the tent, they saw 100 chairs covered in white Satan. Each had a big white bow at the rear of the chair. There were candelabras every fifth row with bright yellow, orange and dark red roses attached. At the front of the tent, there was a raised platform with green Astroturf. It also had candelabras and flowers. The aroma filled the room with sweetness.

Jane said, "This will be perfect for the wedding; but what will we do for the reception?"

Gabritta said, "Nick was very creative on that point. He said that we are to escort the guests back to the chateau after the ceremony and you two kiss. He even had 40 golf carts delivered. We'll have champagne to toast the wedding couple. There will also be hors d'oeuvres. While everyone is congratulating you, the catering firm will be tearing down the chairs and setting up the dance floor, tables, etc. in the tent. Once the musicians arrive and set up, they will start the music. That will be our cue to escort the guests back to the tent."

"I should have known that my man would think of everything."

As the ladies were riding the golf cart back to the chateau, a big truck came through the yard. Gabritta got off the golf cart. She walked up to it and asked, "Do you have the piano in the back of the truck?"

The delivery man answerd, "Yes."

"Wonderful. Back up to the tent and put it on the platform just inside of the entrance."

The delivery man did as he was told. Jane said she wanted to see what he was doing so got out of the golf cart and followed the truck. Once he placed the piano on the platform, she was in awe and yelled to the ladies, "It's a beautiful white baby grand piano. This wedding will go down as one of the best in history."

Marie said quietly to Melina, "I don't think it'll be historical but it will be pretty awesome."

The next day was chaotic. As guests were arriving, they were escorted through the chateau and out to the golf carts. There were many comments about never having ridden on golf carts to a makeshift wedding chapel. As guests entered the tent, Nick's cousin was playing music.

Then the traditional wedding song was played as Jane walked down the isle. She was glowing as she stared at Nick, who was waiting on the raised platform. She had the biggest urge to just run to him but knew that was not protocol.

The wedding went smoothly and everyone waited in the tent while the bridal party went back to the chateau for pictures. More music was played and guests were served the finest wine; and then escorted back to congratulate the happy couple.

Once the caterers had finished setting up for the reception, the music started; and guests were once again escorted back to the tent. A few wives commented to their husbands that it was tasking to keep going back and forth. One husband said, "Would you rather walk in those $3,000 heels across the entire rear of the property or ride in a golf cart?" There was no response.

When Nick heard about the comment, he was going to say something when he gave a toast; but Jane said to keep quiet. "Everything is perfect, Nick. Someone always has to grumble."

As guests departed, the happy couple thanked them for being a part of the momentous occasion. Jane had only met Nick's sister, Agostina, and family previously. She was grateful that many had flown from all parts of the world. Some of Nick's family stayed a few extra days to visit.

While Nick and Jane were in their bedroom preparing for their honeymoon, Jane said, "Let's forget all about that horrific plane crash and your miraculous survival."

"I would love to do that, sweetheart; but this titanium leg attached to my body is a constant reminder. Let's move on, and get to Lake Lucerne for our wonderful honeymoon. However, no plane rides, please. We'll take the train."

With that comment, Jane chuckled and shook her head, yes. Then, they went downstairs, wished everyone a happy visit and left.

Nick said, "I still feel like it's all been a dream. I love you so much, Jane."

Please promise me, that if you take any more plane trips, you'll take me with you."

"That's a promise."

CPSIA information can be obtained
at www.ICGtesting.com
Printed in the USA
FFOW02n1254230318
46046911-46951FF